'What do you w

'You,' Tyler purred.

It was a word he'd have begged to hear in other circumstances. 'Tyler, I...'

She moved towards him. 'Please. Can't we just pretend? I want to go back to the moment when I first walked into your office. Only you're not the private eye my grandmother sent me to. You're just a man and I'm a woman.'

Nick sighed. If this was what Tyler needed right now, he couldn't deny her.

She ran her hand along his chest. 'I've wanted to do this since the first moment I saw you. I felt as if I'd die if I didn't touch you. I felt I might die if I did.'

Her words had his mind clouding, his blood thickening. He wanted to reach for her but he wasn't sure he could lift his arms.

'And then I would have done this.' Rising on her toes, she brushed her lips against his, then pressed tiny kisses against his neck, his chest. 'Once I started, I wouldn't have been able to stop.' She moved her mouth lower. 'And I'm afraid I can't stop now...'

Dear Reader,

What would happen if a happily engaged woman suddenly met Mr Absolutely Wrong—at the right time? That's what happens to my heroine, Tyler Sheridan, when she discovers through 'The Personal Touch!' that her fiancé isn't planning to make an appearance at their wedding.

Writing *Otherwise Engaged* was so much fun! First of all, it allowed me to create the Romano family. They're fun-loving, hardworking and, with the exception of Nick, all great cooks. They remind me a great deal of the Italian side of my own family.

Secondly, it gave me the opportunity to write the kind of story I like best—where two people from very different worlds meet and can't help themselves from falling in love. Nick is a street-smart New York private eye and Tyler's a prim Boston socialite. They never should have met. And they wouldn't have...if not for an ad in 'The Personal Touch!'

I hope you have fun reading about Nick and Tyler's romantic misadventures. I'd love to hear what you think. Write to me at PO Box 327, Dewitt, NY 13214, USA.

Enjoy!

Cara Summers

OTHERWISE ENGAGED

by

Cara Summers

MILLS & BOON®

With love to all my children:
Kevin, Brian and Mary, Brendan and Heather.

And with special thanks to my Dad
and all my Italian relatives who inspired the Romanos.

*First published in Great Britain 2001
by Harlequin Mills & Boon Limited,
Eton House, 18-24 Paradise Road, Richmond, Surrey TW9 1SR*

© Carolyn Hanlon 2001

ISBN 0 263 82821 2

21-1101

*Printed and bound in Spain
by Litografia Rosés S.A., Barcelona*

1

DISASTER. Tyler Sheridan's fingers had started tingling the moment she'd read the ad. They always did when something bad was about to happen. And getting a Dear John letter from her fiancé in the Personals went way beyond bad!

Her first reaction had been to close her eyes and pinch herself. But when she'd finally steeled herself to look again, the ad was still there, the message still the same. That was when the rational part of her brain had kicked in. It had to be a mistake. It was someone's idea of a joke. Richard *couldn't* have placed the ad. She'd just call him and he'd be able to explain.

Sixteen hours later, she'd had to face the fact that Richard James Lawrence, prominent Manhattan accountant, the man she was supposed to marry in a week, couldn't explain anything because he'd disappeared.

She had to get him back! Her whole future as CEO of Sheridan Trust, one of Boston's most prestigious investment firms, depended on finding Richard and convincing him to go through with the wedding. A jilted bride was not going to inspire the confidence of her board of trustees—not when she was already on probation.

The panic bubbling up inside her had sent her to the special file her grandmother had given her just before she died. In it was a business card and a letter of introduction she was supposed to use in just such an emergency. Isabelle Sheridan's exact words had been *"If you want something done quickly and with the utmost secrecy, go to Manhattan and hire Nick Romano."*

But now that she was here and about to enter the offices of Romano Investigations, her fingers had begun to tingle again. Had she come to the right place? The neighborhood wasn't quite as upscale as she'd expected, and the building was old. *Seedy* was the word that came to mind as she'd taken the elevator to the fifth floor, and nothing she saw as she started down the dim hallway dislodged it. Try as she might, she could not picture her grandmother, the strong-minded, impeccably groomed woman who'd ruled Sheridan Trust with an iron hand for thirty years, ever coming to a place like this.

Fishing the business card out of her pocket, she glanced down at the address and once more assured herself that she'd come to the right building, the right floor. No one had answered when she'd called from her hotel, but a recorded voice had informed her the office would open at nine. As she reached the end of the hall, she saw that it hadn't lied. The bold black letters on the frosted glass read N. Romano, Private Investigations. And the door was wide open.

In the light filtering through the broken blinds, Tyler could make out a battered desk with a goose-necked lamp. The scene was suddenly very familiar. Hadn't she seen it before in old movies where the desperate heroine sought out the help of a street-wise private eye? It certainly wasn't a part she'd ever expected to play in real life. And she couldn't imagine Isabelle Sheridan playing it, either.

But Tyler had to find Richard.

Ignoring the fresh wave of tingles in her fingers, she took a deep breath and walked in. A quick glance around told her the room was empty—

Except for the body sprawled full length on the couch. Curious, she moved forward to get a better look.

It was a nearly naked male body. Not able to tear her gaze away, she watched his bare chest rise and fall. Lean and muscled, it was sprinkled with dark hair that narrowed before disappearing beneath the waistband of his bicycle shorts.

She suddenly realized that her fingers had reached out, close enough to nearly brush against that smooth, tan skin, more than close enough to feel its warmth. Snatching her hand back, she fisted it at her side. What in the world was wrong with her? She didn't go around touching strange men. Slowly she drew in a deep breath and let it out as she tried to gather her thoughts.

This couldn't possibly be Nick Romano, could it? She tore her gaze from his body long enough to glance down at the card again. Below the name, she could just make out the words her grandmother had scrawled— "very discrete." Frowning thoughtfully, Tyler let her eyes travel over him again, taking in the lean, roughly handsome face, then lingering again on the tanned skin stretched taut over long bones and muscle.

There was *nothing* discrete about this man. He had the kind of body Italian sculptors had captured over and over again in marble and bronze. Though she'd seen countless pieces in museums, she'd never had a desire to touch any of them.

And she certainly wasn't going to touch this man, either. She was a nearly married woman. *He was a nearly naked man.* Forcing the wayward thought out of her mind, she curled her fingers into fists. It had to be the heat. Manhattan and most of the northeast had been suffering temperatures in the mid-nineties for almost a week, and the air-conditioning drifting in from the hall had lost its battle with the sun pouring through the tall glass windows. It was definitely the heat, she assured herself as a nasty drip of sweat made its way down her back. But she couldn't seem to rid herself of the sensation that something about this man was reaching out to her, tugging at her....

She wanted to move forward almost as much as she wanted to run.

Sheridans never run. Drawing in a deep breath, Tyler repeated the words in her head and stood her ground. If this was indeed Nick Romano, she needed his help. If he wasn't, he was the only person around who could tell her that. Either way she had to handle him. No, handle the *situation.* She'd solved worse problems in the Sheridan Trust boardroom, hadn't she?

Suddenly, she had it! Every modern corporate CEO was trained in visualization techniques. She'd just put some clothes on him—a dark gray suit, white shirt, a deeper gray in the striped tie... Slowly the picture formed in her mind. Only then did she clear her throat and say, "Excuse me—"

He shot up and off the couch, his hand whipping around to his back. Tyler took one quick step in retreat before she could stop herself. He was reaching for a gun. She was sure of it, even though his hand came up empty. And a gun would have been easier to face than this man's eyes. Dark and potent, they sliced into her and dried up her throat.

Then, as suddenly as it had appeared, the fierceness faded. His gaze narrowed. In that same instant she became aware of how close they were standing. He was larger now that he was standing up. And somehow in that leap off the couch, the clothes she'd pictured him in had fallen off.

Sheridans never run. She clung to the thought while the two stood motionless, facing each other.

"You didn't knock," he finally said.

Tyler swallowed. In a minute, just as soon as her system leveled, she was going to have to put those clothes right back on him again. "The door was wide open. I'm looking for Nick Romano."

"Well, you found him, sugar—"

But it wasn't until he glanced past her that Tyler let out the rest of the breath she'd been holding.

"And the only reason that door was open was because I was hoping that some of the air-conditioning would drift in from the hall."

Tyler looked at the unit filling one of the windows. "Why didn't you just turn yours on?"

"The electricity's been shut off," he said.

For the first time she noticed the file drawers, open and empty, the boxes stacked neatly against the wall.

"You're moving?" she asked, turning back to him with a frown.

"That's right."

"That would explain your clothes, I suppose."

He glanced down at himself, and when his gaze once more returned to hers, the amusement was clear. "Something wrong?"

Tyler's brows rose. "You'll have to admit, even for a dress-down Friday, they're a little skimpy."

Nick grinned. "Very funny. The truth is, I was think-

ing of taking a run, but it was hot and the couch called
out to me."

Tyler found herself staring as the warmth of his smile
lit his face, transforming him into the antithesis of the
warrior who'd sprung off the couch. She found herself
wanting to smile right back at him. But the moment he
took a step toward her, she drew herself up and focused. "The case I want you to take is urgent. In addition to your fee, I'll cover whatever it will cost to re-
schedule the movers."

"No."

The grin had faded, but she still had the distinct feeling he was laughing at her. Moving to the desk, she
took her checkbook out of her purse and uncapped her
pen. "I'm not making myself clear. You can name your
fee."

"No."

She jumped when he touched her. His grip was gentle, firm, and she was very much aware of the press of
each one of his fingers on the inside of her arm. So
aware that she didn't realize her feet were moving until
she found that he'd led her into the hallway.

"Look, lady, let's start over." His tone was patient,
controlled, reminding her of any one of several nannies
she'd had before she'd been shipped off to boarding
school.

She wanted to slap him.

"Let's pretend you've just come up in the elevator,"
Nick continued, "and when you got here, the door was
shut. You knocked, but there was no answer because
Romano Investigations closed shop last night at 5:00
p.m. You missed hiring me by about fifteen hours. I can
recommend my cousin Sam. He used to work for me,
and he just got a job with a big security firm uptown.

See—" he tapped a finger on the door "—I taped one of his business cards right here." Ripping it free, he handed it to her. "He'll be happy to take your money."

Tyler watched, stunned, as he shut the door of his office in her face. She heard the lock click, then his footsteps growing fainter. She very much wanted to give the door a good, swift kick. But she didn't. Sheridans didn't kick doors. That had been drilled into her by the time she was three. She wanted to scream, too. That phase had lasted until she was five.

But worst of all, she wanted to cry. She could feel the hot needle-like pricks burning at the back of her eyes. She hadn't cried since she was eleven. Not even at her grandmother's funeral six months ago. Taking a deep breath, she blinked away the dampness. Nick Romano was not going to make her cry. So what if he'd closed shop. He could just open it up again. She had to get him to help her. There was no one else.

She had taken two steps toward the closed door, her hand raised to knock, when her cell phone rang. Only two people had her number: Naomi Prescott, her personal assistant, and Richard. *Please, God, let it be Richard.* Unsnapping her purse, she grabbed the phone and flipped it open. "Yes?"

"Tyler, Naomi gave me your number. She tells me you flew to New York last night. Is everything all right?"

Howard. Drawing in a deep breath, Tyler struggled to keep the disappointment out of her voice. "Everything's fine, Howard."

Howard Tremaine was her mother's fourth husband, the third that Claudia Tyler Sheridan had chosen to marry since Tyler's father had died, and the only one who'd shown an interest in working at Sheridan Trust.

He'd appointed himself her personal advisor ever since she'd stepped into her grandmother's shoes.

"You'd tell me if something was going wrong with the Bradshaw deal? I could be on the next plane."

"Everything is right on schedule." Tyler sent up another quick prayer. Sheridan Trust had been pursuing Bradshaw Enterprises for months before her grandmother died, but Tyler had been the one to convince Hamilton Bradshaw to come aboard. The papers were to be signed at a family dinner at his Manhattan apartment on Sunday. Richard was supposed to escort her. Howard and her mother were to be there too, because Hamilton Bradshaw had a fondness for family-run companies.

"And you're sure that everything is all right between you and Richard? He was supposed to fly in last night, wasn't he?"

"Richard and I are fine, Howard. I just decided it would be easier to play hooky if I flew to Manhattan. Certainly a bride and groom have the right to do that eight days before the wedding."

"Playing hooky?" He gave an audible sigh. "Well, I'm delighted to hear it. I think it's great you've decided to relax a little. I was afraid that you might have had some kind of lover's quarrel, or, worse still, that you'd decided to elope and cheat us all out of the elegant bash your mother has planned next Saturday."

Tyler made herself smile, hoping it would show in her voice. "No, it's nothing like that, Howard. Richard and I have never quarreled. And if I eloped, it would tarnish the image you've been helping me create for the board of trustees. They'd pull the plug on me even before my year's probation is up. Besides, Hamilton Bradshaw is planning on attending the wedding. I wouldn't want him disappointed in Sheridan Trust before he has time to settle in."

Even as she spoke, a totally different image formed in her mind. It was a scene she'd watched hundreds of times in movies. Papers were rolling off the presses, the music was swelling, and there she was on the cover of the *Boston Globe* in her bridal dress and veil, waiting at the altar alone. Above her the headline screamed, *Tyler Sheridan, Acting CEO of Sheridan Trust, Jilted!*

"Tyler...are you still there?"

Tyler swallowed the tight ball of panic lodged in her throat. "Yes?"

"I thought I lost you for a moment. Tell Richard to give me a call later. I have some last-minute bachelor party things to go over with him. I'll cover for you here."

"Thanks, Howard. 'Bye."

For just a moment, Tyler let herself lean against the wall. Howard was one of the few people at Sheridan Trust who had given her his unquestioning support since her grandmother's death. And his interest in working at Sheridan Trust had brought her mother back to Boston. Tyler had begun to hope that the rift between her mother and grandmother would eventually heal. For fourteen years, ever since Tyler's father had died, Claudia and Isabelle had blamed each other for his death.

Still, she couldn't tell Howard, she couldn't tell anyone yet that Richard was missing. The only person she could confide in was Nick Romano. If her grandmother said he could be trusted, he could. She had to believe that. There was no other choice. In a minute, just as soon as she was in control, she was going to make him help her.

WITH ONE QUICK SWEEP of his arm, Nick scooped everything on his desk into a box. He'd done the right thing. So why the hell did he feel like he'd kicked a defenseless puppy? Pulling out a drawer, he dumped it unceremoniously into the next box.

That woman was not defenseless. He knew the type—a spoiled rich girl, swimming in inherited wealth and certain that it could buy her anything she wanted. His sisters and his mother would have admired the style of that neat little suit she wore. His own taste ran to her legs. They were first class, just like the rest of her. And in spite of the heat, she'd looked picture perfect, not one strand of that pale-gold hair out of place, not one wrinkle in her clothes. Nothing loose, nothing unbuttoned. At any other time, he'd have been tempted to muss her up a bit. Just thinking about it made his lips curve.

Propping a hip against the side of his desk, Nick let his gaze return to the door. She'd been young too, not more than twenty-four or five. And there'd been that flash of fear he'd seen in her eyes when he'd leapt off the couch. In spite of it, she hadn't run and she hadn't screamed.

Courage. He'd always been a sucker for it. Nick glanced at the phone. She couldn't have left the building yet. There was a chance he could still catch—

No. He stopped himself before he could start for the door. No way. Little Miss Picture Perfect was the last thing he needed right now. He was out of the PI business for good. After ten years, the cage door had finally swung open.

His job with a law firm in L.A. would finally allow him to achieve his dream of practicing law. Though he'd received his degree over a year ago, he had yet to put it to any use in Manhattan. There was always one last investigation to finish, one last favor to do before he could close his office. In California, no one need ever know he'd been a P.I. for ten years. No one would seek him out and beg him to take just one last case. Rising, he walked over to his computer and pulled the plug out of the wall, then out of the machine. As he coiled it and dropped it in an open box, he concentrated on the new life that was waiting for him out in California. His mother's boutique was making a steady profit, and between that and what he'd be able to send her each month, his two sisters would make it through college. He was a free man!

The phone rang. Nick sent it a frown. He had a pretty good idea who it was. The smart thing to do was let it ring, let his answering machine pick it up. But he reached for it all the same. "Romano here."

"You didn't let me introduce myself. I'm Tyler Sheridan."

Nick heard the warning bell ringing in the back of his mind. "So?"

"My grandmother was Isabelle Sheridan of Sheridan Trust in Boston. You did some work for her. She said I could trust you. I have a letter of introduction in my purse."

Nick scowled first at the phone, then at the door. Why in hell had he left it open? Turning, he glared at the couch. If he hadn't fallen asleep—

"Mr. Romano, are you still there?"

"Yeah." A few hours later and he wouldn't have been. He'd have missed Miss Tyler Sheridan completely. Why was it that today of all days, the past had to reach out and grab him?

"Could you please let me in? My business is private."

Hanging up the phone, Nick walked to the door. The fact that she was Isabelle Sheridan's granddaughter changed nothing, he told himself. The promise he'd made had concerned the old lady. Any obligation had ended when she'd died. Opening the door, he said, "I was sorry to hear about your grandmother's death."

"Thank you."

She moved past him quickly, but not before he'd seen the pain flash into her eyes. Isabelle had died six months ago, but this woman was still grieving. With a silent sigh, Nick closed the door. He knew how hard it was to lose family.

"How much should I make the check out for?"

"Forget about the check." Even as he said the words, he discovered that it was much easier to refuse the spoiled rich girl than the woman who'd lost her grandmother. He'd read about Isabelle Sheridan's sudden death in the papers. And he'd also glanced through several profiles written about the young woman who was standing before him, the woman Isabelle had personally groomed to take her place at the head of a multibillion-dollar investment firm. Only, the old lady hadn't planned on dying so soon, because Tyler Sheridan looked much too young for the job. "Look, I'm not in the PI business anymore. I have a new job in L.A that starts next week. The best I can do for you is escort you to my cousin Sam's office and personally introduce you. He's the best—"

"I want you. My grandmother said in an emergency to use you—no one else. I can't afford to share any of this with a stranger."

"Why don't you use the security firm in Boston that your grandmother used?" Nick asked.

"Because my business is...personal, and my— This problem is here in Manhattan."

Her voice had tightened slightly, and her knuckles had turned white where they were gripping her purse. Those were the only signs that beneath that cool, un-flappable exterior, she was wound tight. Contrasts had always intrigued him. Once again Nick fought against his weakening resolve. "Let me see if I can guess. You want me to tail your boyfriend and see if he's cheating on you?"

Two bright spots of color stained her cheeks. "I'm not going to discuss the case until you agree to take it." Then suddenly her eyes widened. "That can't be the only kind of work you do. I'm sure that's not the kind of work you did for my grandmother—"

He saw the flash of doubt in her eyes and the curiosity.

"Was it?"

"I never talk about any of my client's cases."

After a second, she nodded. "Good. Okay. I have to trust you not to talk about mine."

Nick's eyes narrowed. She might be young, but he was beginning to see how effectively she might operate in a board room, and he wished he didn't admire her for it. "I haven't agreed to take your case."

Tyler met his eyes steadily. "Will you?"

"You're as stubborn as your grandmother."

"I'll take that as a compliment."

He grinned grudgingly. "She would have, too."

Once again, he saw pain in her eyes, and his curiosity increased. "You mentioned a letter of introduction?"

Unsnapping her purse, she extracted it and handed it to him. Nick regretted asking for it the moment he read it: "'Nicholas, if you read this, then it means that I am no longer here and my granddaughter needs your help. Your promise to your uncle ended with my death, but listen to what she has to say and don't judge her by my mistakes. Belle.'"

"Damn!" He glanced up in time to see the corners of her mouth twitch. "Something funny?"

"No. My grandmother's missives are seldom funny. 'Damn' usually sums them up quite well."

He studied her for a moment, knowing that his decision had already been made. "I'll take the case on one condition—if I can't wind everything up by Tuesday, you'll let me refer you to my cousin. I'm flying to L.A. on Wednesday morning."

Tyler hesitated for a moment.

"Take it or leave it," Nick said.

"Agreed."

He walked to his desk and sat down on the corner. "Okay, what's the problem?"

"I'm getting married next Saturday, and my fiancé has disappeared. I want you to find him."

For a second, Nick said nothing. She was the coolest looking jilted bride he'd ever seen. He watched her as she unsnapped her purse.

"The last time I heard from him—"

"Wait. I can save us both some time here. If your bridegroom has bolted, don't waste your money. Just let him go."

Her eyes snapped up to his and narrowed. "I didn't come here for advice. And he's my *fiancé*. He won't be my bridegroom until next Saturday."

Nick waved a hand. "Fiancé, bridegroom. We could sit around and debate word choice all day but—" he lifted the clock off his filing cabinet "—the clock is ticking."

"That one isn't," she pointed out.

Nick glanced down at it and frowned. "Damn. I forgot the electricity was turned off. No wonder it didn't go off. If it had, you'd have missed me completely."

"Must be my lucky day," Tyler said.

Nick glanced at her. "Good one." No, she definitely wasn't a defenseless puppy. And he was becoming certain she wasn't simply the spoiled rich girl he'd thought at first. That intrigued him even more than the fabulous legs. With some effort, he kept himself from looking at them again. "Okay, back to the missing bridegroom."

"Fiancé. Words *are* important. I like to use them accurately."

"Believe me, sugar, any man who is within a week of his wedding has started to think of himself as a groom. He can picture himself in that monkey suit, the tie cutting off his oxygen supply, and that ball and chain rolling inexorably toward him, ready to snap its jaws tight around his ankle. If your husband-to-be is missing, it's more likely than not he's got a classic case of cold feet and taken a powder. And with the divorce rate the way it is today, you don't need a bridegroom who's having second thoughts."

Tyler strode toward him until they were standing toe to toe. "And I don't need to hire a PI who's going to waste my time. Is that all they taught you in detective school—to jump to conclusions and argue?"

"Jeez," Nick said, putting a hand over his heart, "you really know how to hurt a guy."

Tyler's chin lifted. "My grandmother said you could be trusted. She didn't say you were any good. Are you?"

"Sugar, I'm a regular Sherlock Holmes." Reaching quickly, he snagged her hand. When she tried to pull away, he held tight. "That was a pretty direct challenge. Bear with me for a moment. This is your engagement ring?"

"Yes."

"He chose it, right?"

"Yes, but—"

"No, don't say another word. Let me show you what I learned in detective school. You would have chosen something a little smaller, more conservative, I think...perhaps something with a different stone in the setting, a sapphire to match your eyes." He glanced up, saw that he had her attention, and went on. "The size of the stone tells me that he wanted to impress you or your family. That means the money he has is new, not the kind that's been handed down to him. He wanted to make sure you knew he could measure up. He's a little nervous about this wedding." Nick paused, then asked, "How am I doing so far?"

"You're guessing."

Nick smiled. "Detectives have to make guesses. Good ones guess right. I'm also betting that he works in a business that your board of trustees would approve of—banking, the stock market...no, accounting. I'll bet he's an accountant."

Her eyes widened. "How could you possibly know that?"

"From you. Seems to me that's the type you'd go for, someone who would know all the facts, figures, the bottom line. Someone who could make everything add up right, just the way you add up nice and neat until I get to your eyes."

It was a mistake to look into them for too long, Nick realized. The color reminded him of the glass bowl that sat in his mother's china cabinet, hand blown by his father years ago in Venice—except her eyes were an even deeper blue, violet almost, contrasting sharply with the porcelain fairness of her skin. He felt a sudden urge to brush his fingertips along the curve of her cheek. Could she possibly feel as cool as she looked? If he touched her right now, could he make the fire leap back into her eyes?

The phone rang, and Nick dropped Tyler's hand, then reached automatically for the receiver. Still, there was a tiny span of time when he couldn't seem to drag his eyes away from her, when his mind seemed to be completely blank. His mother was in mid-sentence before her voice finally penetrated.

"Mama," he said, finally shifting his eyes away from Tyler's. "No, Rosa's fiancé is not cheating on her. I hate to say I told you so, but I— How do I *know*? Because I'm the world's best..."

Tyler tore her gaze away from Nick and focused on the door to the office behind him. As soon as she felt sure she wouldn't stumble, she took two careful steps back from his desk. Pride prevented her from taking any more. But standing close to this man had the strangest effect on her senses. He'd only been holding her hand, but for a moment she'd imagined his fingertips brushing along her cheekbone, then down her throat to where her jacket buttoned, and she'd wanted...

Giving her head a quick shake, Tyler tried to get rid of the image of Nick Romano unbuttoning her jacket, slipping the sleeves down her arms. Ruthlessly, she pushed the picture out of her mind, but she could still feel the heat licking along her nerve endings before it arrowed deeper. What in the world was wrong with her? She'd never fantasized about a man touching her before. Not even Richard.

Richard. The heat inside her tightened into a cold ball of fear and settled in her stomach. It was Richard she should be thinking of. Not this dangerous half-naked man sitting in front of her. No, she had to stop thinking of him as half naked. Mentally, she began to dress him again. This time in brown oxfords, a tweed coat with a cape, and a hat. At the last moment she added a pipe, but he still didn't look like any Sherlock Holmes she'd ever seen.

Nick jumped up, muttering something in Italian, then threw back his head and laughed. "Okay, okay, I'll give it to you straight. Carlo's moonlighting, working a second job. How do I *know*? You're tough, Mama. My paying clients don't grill me like this. I tailed him all night long from one end of the Bronx to the other. I even followed him to his door this morning."

Laughing with his mother, Nick Romano didn't look dangerous at all. Had Sherlock Holmes ever laughed? Tyler wondered. Richard seldom did. She frowned at the thought, wondering where it had come from. Richard didn't have to laugh. He was everything she'd ever wanted in a husband, and she had to find him. The fear in her stomach tightened again. Could Nick Romano be right? Could Richard's disappearance merely be due to a bad case of wedding jitters? She really wanted to believe it could be that simple. But in the hours she'd spent searching for Richard, she'd become increasingly sure that something much worse was going on.

"Mama, I gotta go. No, I'm not entertaining a lady in my office. Well—" he glanced at Tyler "—she's definitely a lady, but she doesn't find me entertaining. She's a client. It's a long story, Mamma, longer than solving the case is going to take. No. Nothing has changed. I'm still flying to L.A. on Wednesday. Uh huh. Love you, too," he added as he replaced the receiver. Then he turned to face Tyler. "Okay, tell me, when was the last time you saw your bridegroom?"

"When I drove him to Logan Airport last Sunday. He's been flying into Boston every weekend to take care of last-minute details for the wedding. Everything was fine until yesterday afternoon."

"Yesterday? You mean he hasn't even been missing a whole day yet?"

"He was supposed to fly in to Boston last night. He was taking Friday off so that we could spend some time together that wasn't focused on wedding preparations. I met every single plane that flew into Logan from Manhattan."

"Maybe he had to work late. Have you checked at his office?"

"I called them yesterday afternoon. They said he was taking a few days off. I know how that sounds...."

"It sounds like there's no panic on *their* part," Nick said.

"No, but that doesn't mean—" Stopping short, she narrowed her eyes. "Shouldn't you be taking notes or something?"

Nick grinned at her as he tapped his temple with one finger. "No need. I have a superb memory."

"Sorry. I forgot for a moment I was dealing with Sherlock Holmes."

Nick bit back a laugh. Beauty, brains, great legs *and* a sense of humor. It was just too damn bad that her last name was Sheridan. "Look, maybe he's just playing hooky by himself. Why don't we check his apartment."

"I did that on my way here, right after I checked into the Plaza."

Nick listened as she detailed her search of her bridegroom's apartment. She'd covered all the bases, even checking to see if he'd packed a suitcase. He hadn't, but that didn't necessarily mean anything. Nick was still convinced that Tyler Sheridan's bridegroom had gotten a case of cold feet. The problem was that his thumbs had started to prick. They always did when something was wrong.

"I know what it all sounds like," Tyler said as she opened her purse again. "And I know what this looks like, but—"

"Hold on. Before you write that check...have you stopped to consider that he might be with his family?"

"His family?"

"You know—Mom, Dad, siblings. Maybe he's just gone home for the weekend."

"Richard never talks about his family. He hasn't seen them in years."

"Well, it's possible he's decided to change all that. Weddings are a good opportunity to patch things up. Why don't you give them a call?"

Tyler frowned. "I don't know where they live."

Nick's brows rose. "You didn't invite them to the wedding?"

"He said they wouldn't come. I never thought... Maybe that *is* where he's gone."

"It's worth a shot." Lifting the receiver, Nick dialed a number. "My cousin Sam is a genius with computers. He can get into any database that's been created." He spoke into the phone. "Sam, I need a favor... Yeah, I know I've retired. But I've got a missing persons case and I need to trace his parents." With a grin, he said,

"Yeah, the client is a *she*, and she's very pretty. Here, I'll let you talk to her." As he handed Tyler the phone, he said, "You can trust him."

The moment she began to talk into the phone, Nick walked over to the window and tried to ignore a twinge of guilt.

It was *possible* that Richard had gone home to reconcile with his family. But Nick didn't think so. Not that it would hurt to have Sam trace the parents. By the time, they discovered that Richard wasn't with them, Tyler might be more accepting of the truth. And she'd find it out earlier than a lot of brides did—eight whole days before the wedding.

In the meantime, he could hold her hand, get her through a rough time. What could be the harm in that?

A lot, warned the nagging little voice in his mind. Turning back to her, Nick recalled the feeling he'd had earlier when he'd looked into her eyes, the almost overpowering need he'd felt to touch her. And he knew that he'd feel it again. Tyler Sheridan was...different.

She came from a different world, he reminded himself. *Like her grandmother before her.* The safest course would be to escort her back to her hotel and keep in touch by phone. Then Tyler turned back to him and looked into his eyes. He felt the punch right down to his toes. Hell, when had he ever taken the safe course?

"It'll take Sam at least an hour or so," he said. "Why don't I pull on some clothes and I'll take you to lunch?"

"I'm not hungry," Tyler said. "And there's something that I haven't shown you yet." She unsnapped her purse. "This was delivered to my office late yesterday afternoon via special messenger."

Nick glanced down at the glossy magazine she'd handed him. It was folded open to a page of personal ads. He read aloud the one that was circled: "'TMS, Sorry I'll miss the wedding. I'll be in touch. Remember Scarlet and Annie. RJL.'"

"The magazine came out yesterday," Tyler said.

"You think you're TMS and Richard is RJL?"

"Yes. I *know* it's from Richard. He's sent me messages before using these Personals. I...it's sort of a private joke. We never would have met if I hadn't placed a personal ad in this magazine."

"Wait. Time out. Are you saying that you got engaged to someone by running an ad in the—" he glanced down at the magazine again "—the Personal Touch column?"

"No. Not exactly. It's a long story, and it hardly matters now. I know what the ad looks like. It looks like proof that he's gotten cold feet." She moved forward then to touch him, a hand on his arm. "I know it's more than that. Something is wrong. I just feel it."

Nick felt it, too. His thumbs were pricking like crazy. And then there was the fact that his skin had begun to heat beneath her hand. More worrisome was the ache, a very dull ache that was building right in his center. Stepping away, he grabbed a T-shirt and put it on, then pulled jeans on over his shorts. "C'mon," he said, urging her toward the door as he slipped on his shoes.

"Where are we—"

"We're going to see if we can find out who placed this ad and when. Then we'll have lunch."

2

TYLER WATCHED as the polar bear dove toward her, turned, planted its feet firmly against the pane of glass separating it from the crowd of onlookers and pushed itself back to the surface. Then it turned and dove toward her again. In the short time she'd been watching, it hadn't tired of executing over and over the same set of incredibly graceful movements: plunging down to the glass, turning, pushing off, and shooting to the surface. She found the performance every bit as fascinating as did the children pressed against the guardrail.

When the bear finally took a break and joined its companion on the bank, Tyler glanced over her shoulder and checked on Nick's progress at the vending cart. In the taxi on the way over, he'd informed her that they'd grab something to eat in the park. It would eliminate a wait for a table, and he wouldn't have to worry about dress codes. Then, since he'd already canceled his service, he'd commandeered her cell phone so he could make it a working lunch. He was talking on it even now, as he pulled bills out of a worn-looking wallet.

The man had contacts everywhere, it seemed—from a good buddy who just happened to head up security at the Plaza Hotel where she was staying, to an ex-girlfriend who had a contact at *Attitudes Magazine* where the personal ad had run.

She continued to study him as he shoved the phone

in his pocket and began to chat with the woman running the vending cart. Richard would never take the time to do that. Nor would he ever have considered lunching on hot dogs in Central Park.

The two men were so different. Richard was meticulously groomed and very selective about his wardrobe, while Nick's approach to both seemed haphazard, reckless even. Her gaze dropped to the jeans he'd pulled on, which were fraying at several strategic spots. Recklessness was something she'd avoided all of her life. That thought was still on her mind when she glanced up and met his eyes. For one full moment, she felt the same way she had in his office. The children's laughter, the pungent smell of the animals, the sounds of the traffic—everything around her seemed to fade. All she could think of was him.

No, she thought as the quick skip of panic moved through her. She could not possibly be attracted to this man. He wasn't her type. Richard was. And Richard would be good for her, she told herself again. His gaze slipped away from her then, as he pulled out her cell phone. A second later, he was gesturing dramatically with his hands.

Tyler drew in a deep breath and let it out. But she didn't feel the relief she wanted. What was it about Nick Romano that he could pull a response from her she couldn't control? If she was going to work with him, she would have to figure it out.

At the back of her mind the old questions hammered. Had her grandmother been right? Was Tyler her mother's daughter, after all? Isabelle had always told her she had to fight against the passionate side of her nature that she'd inherited from her mother. And passion had definitely ruled Claudia. Otherwise, why would she have married again barely a year after Tyler's father had died? And why would she have left Tyler with Isabelle, then flitted from one husband to the next?

Drawing in a deep breath, Tyler pushed the questions away. She wasn't going to let the old self-doubts creep in. And she would figure out a way to handle Nick Romano...and find Richard.

Turning back to the polar bear, she made herself focus on the dive—down to the glass, then back to the surface; down to the glass, back to the surface. Gradually, the rhythm of the movements soothed her. She imagined herself diving with him, feeling the coolness of the water slipping over her skin, then hit the solid barrier of glass. Was he hoping to escape? Did he believe that perhaps this time it would give and he would be free?

"Well, what do you think of the Central Park Zoo's main attraction?" Nick asked as he joined her.

"I think they should take him back to the North Pole and set him free," she said without hesitation.

Nick studied her for a moment. "You surprise me, sugar. If it makes you feel any better, he probably wouldn't survive if they did."

He was carrying a loaded paper tray, and she grabbed for the napkins as they began to blow away. "Nobody should be trapped like that."

"A few years ago, he might have agreed with you. All he used to do was repeat that dive, over and over and over. The zoo people finally called in a psychiatrist."

Tyler looked at him. "You're joking."

"Absolutely not." He nudged her toward a bench. "The big fella was diagnosed with one of those obsessive compulsive disorders. I swear," he assured her when she shot him a skeptical look. "If I'm lying, may I never take a bite of my mama's cooking again."

"Can your mother cook?" asked Tyler as she sat down.

"Ouch. It's a good thing I have a thick skin. I would never lie about my mother's cooking."

"All right. I'll bite. What did the psychiatrist say?"

"Claimed our polar bear needed companionship," Nick said as he joined her on the bench. "So they got him a girlfriend, and the big fella no longer devotes *all* of his time to diving."

Tyler looked back at the exhibit. "It's still a trap. The only difference is that two of them are in it now."

Nick shook his head sadly. "A bride eight days away from her wedding, and she doesn't believe in romance."

"Oh, yes, I do," Tyler insisted. "I just don't believe in getting carried away by it."

"Where's the fun if you don't get carried away a little?" Nick asked, then held out the tray. "Dig in. Yours is the naked one. Beats me how you can bear to eat a hot dog that way."

"It's an old habit."

"Time to break it. The best thing about a hot dog is the toppings." As he bit into his, chili splatted onto his jeans.

A laugh bubbled up before she could stop it. "Sorry," she said, as he used a napkin to dab at his knee. "That's why I eat them plain. Otherwise..." She glanced up and found her face close to his, their eyes and lips perfectly aligned. The rest of her thought slipped away as something moved through her to her very core, then tugged. It was what she'd felt before, when he'd been holding her hand in his office, and it took all of her control not to jerk herself back out of range. Slowly, carefully, she straightened.

"Otherwise...?" Nick prompted.

"Disaster," she murmured as her fingers began to tingle.

"*Disaster* is a pretty strong word for a little spilled chili."

Tyler forced her mind back to what they'd been talking about. "I'd never spill just a little. I'd be a mess."

"It's hard to imagine you any way but perfectly neat and tidy," Nick said.

She smiled. "You should have seen me when I was younger. My grandmother would take me to a Red Sox game every summer when I would come to visit. By the seventh inning, I'd have more mustard and ketchup on me than there was on the hot dog. Then she'd lecture me on how Sheridans never spilled their food and never, ever appeared in public without being perfectly groomed. It was either give up the toppings or the Red Sox."

"I'd have given up the Red Sox."

Surprised, she looked at him.

"Now," he continued, "if it was a choice between a chili dog and the Yankees, that would be a different story. Here—" He offered her his chili dog. "You're a big girl now. Live dangerously."

She found it was impossible to resist the challenge in his eyes. Leaning forward, she took a bite and savored the explosion of flavors on her tongue. "Mmm. Wonderful."

"There you go," Nick said. "You've sampled the forbidden and you're none the worse for it. I'd say you're pretty mess proof. In fact, you remind me of one of Hitchcock's heroines. Even when they were whipping around in convertibles, their hair never got wind-blown."

Tyler gave him a level look. "That's because those scenes were shot in a studio. The cars never moved."

"Safer, I suppose, but not nearly as satisfying." Reaching over, he fingered the gold loop on her ear. "Wouldn't you rather take a real ride in a very fast car?"

"No." *Not until now.* Tyler frowned as the thought moved through her mind. It was as traitorous as the feeling that had moved through her when he'd touched her earring. And it wasn't even true. She had her life just the way she wanted it. She didn't want rides in fast cars. And she didn't want the feelings that Nick Romano could trigger in her. "That's not who I am. That's not how I've achieved what I have. I've worked very hard to get where I am at Sheridan Trust. It means everything to me."

Nick studied her for a minute. "It's got to be hard filling your grandmother's shoes. Even if she thought you could do it, I imagine there are some who doubt her judgment."

At the understanding she saw in his eyes, panic moved through her. "*Maybe* you are a good detective," Tyler said.

Nick sighed and shook his head. "I can see it's going to be an uphill battle trying to impress you."

"Believe it," she said as she bit into her hot dog. For a few minutes they ate in silence. Tyler tried to ignore that hers tasted bland. Over the years, she'd schooled herself not to notice that. Swallowing, she wrapped what remained in a napkin and took a sip of her bottled water. "Did you find out if Richard placed the want ad?"

"It's hard to say," Nick said around a mouthful of chili dog. "According to the records, Richard placed the earlier ads over the phone with a credit card. The man who placed the one in this issue came to the magazine's offices in person and paid cash. The girl who took the ad couldn't recall much about his appearance. Medium height, medium build, brown hair."

"That could be Richard."

"And about one-third of all the other men who live in Manhattan, not to mention the tourists. The thing she was most sure about was that she took the ad on Monday. That was the deadline for placing anything in this month's issue. The arrangements with the messenger service were made yesterday. That's when the magazine gets mailed to subscribers."

Tyler frowned. "But if he placed the ad Monday, then he knew four days ago that he was going to disappear."

"Yeah. *If* Richard was the one who placed it." Balling up the remnants of their lunch, Nick took aim and tossed it into the trash container.

"I know that Richard placed that ad. He's the only one who could have composed it," Tyler said. "No one else would know about Scarlet and Annie."

"I was going to ask you about that. Who are they?"

"Scarlet O'Hara and Little Orphan Annie. *Gone with the Wind* is his favorite movie and *Annie* is his favorite musical. It was something we had in common."

"He really liked *Gone with the Wind*?"

"Yes. Didn't you?"

Nick shrugged. "I don't think I've ever seen it all the way through. It certainly wouldn't make my top-ten list." He turned to her then to study her. "So, Scarlet and Annie are your favorites?" Reaching over, he again fingered the loop of gold at her ear.

Tyler drew in a deep breath and let it out, trying to ignore her racing heart. "I want you to stop that."

Nick dropped his hand. "It bothers you?"

"No, of course not. It's just...that is...I don't like people to violate my personal space."

"Really?"

She couldn't for the life of her figure out how he could have such a sober expression on his face, such a serious tone to his voice, and at the same time be laughing at her with his eyes. But she was *not* going to give in to the urge to punch him. "Really. Are we clear on that?"

"Absolutely. Hands off." He raised both of his. "And I do approve."

"Of what?" she asked suspiciously.

"Your personal favorites. Scarlet and Annie. You're a little like both of them. They're determined and they are both full of surprises."

Tyler gave him another level look. "So are Hitchcock heroines, in spite of their perfect hairdos. While the men in those movies, as I recall, are always a bit befuddled."

Nick threw back his head and laughed. The sound was so rich and free that several heads turned their way, and Tyler found herself wanting to join him.

"Good one," he finally said. "Do you deliver zingers like that in your board meetings?"

"No," she said.

"Well, you should. They'd start to think twice before they crossed you. C'mon," he said, rising from the bench. "Let's take a walk. I think better when I'm on the move." He led the way, cutting a path between two women pushing strollers. To their left, a group of children stared wide-eyed at penguins, and the penguins stared right back. Farther ahead, seals clapped and preened themselves in an enclosed fountain while water shot high into the air.

"So, how about telling me the long story about why your bridegroom used the personal ads to send you little messages."

When Tyler didn't immediately reply, he continued, "Look, if you want my help, I need to know everything. It won't go any farther. I never rat out my clients. Besides, I'm dying to know why someone like you would have to place an ad in the Personals?"

"I did it because my college roommate dared me."

Nick stared at her. "Would you jump off a cliff on a dare?"

"No, but you don't know Stevie. She was always after me to date. So was my mother. I figured the responses to an ad in the Personals couldn't be any worse than the men my mother was always inviting to dinner."

"So under pressure from your college roommate and your mother, you took out an ad in the Personals." He studied her for a moment. "I can understand maternal pressure. So far mine has stopped short of encouraging me to advertise."

When they reached the guardrail surrounding the seals, Nick paused and leaned against it. One of the seals was cleverly balancing a ball on its nose. Nearby, a toddler laughed delightedly.

"He should take that act on the road," Nick said, slanting her a grin.

"Speaking of being on the road—shouldn't we be going somewhere or doing something besides wandering through the zoo?" Tyler asked.

"We are," Nick said. "We're waiting for reports. Ten percent of PI work is setting things in motion. Eighty percent is waiting for the results."

"And the other ten?"

Nick grinned. "Catching the bad guys."

"I'd prefer to do something besides wait. Shouldn't you make a plan?"

"I can't until I have more information. And then there might not be time for one. A good PI has to live in the now."

Tyler's brows rose. "Is that what we're doing right now?"

"Yep." He tapped his temple. "Plus, we're theorizing. Any thoughts on why your bridegroom used a want ad for sending a Dear John letter?"

Tyler shook her head. "How about you?"

Nick shrugged. "Phone calls and e-mails can be traced. So far we haven't been able to trace the want ad. The question is—why is he being so secretive?"

Tyler searched his face. "Does this mean that you don't think he's a runaway bridegroom anymore?"

"Nope. It just means that I'm keeping an open mind and trying to explore all the possibilities. That's another thing they teach us in detective school." Suddenly his expression grew serious. "You ought to keep an open mind, too. Just in case my initial theory pans out."

The concern in his eyes was genuine. It surprised her in much the same way his expression of sympathy about her grandmother had. Drawing in a deep breath, she said, "I've thought about it, but I can't believe Richard would just take off. I know—" she raised a hand to stop him from speaking "—you think I'm just being too stubborn to face the possibility, but it's more than that. Richard was the one who pushed for an early wedding date. I wanted to wait until...until I was sure...."

When she paused, Nick said, "You weren't sure of your feelings for him?"

She shook her head. "No, I was sure about wanting to marry Richard. I just wanted to wait until my future at Sheridan Trust was...settled."

Nick studied her. "I thought you were the new boss."

Turning, Tyler rested her arms on the guardrail and concentrated on keeping her tone even. "I have a year to prove myself to the board of directors. My grandmother's illness was quite sudden, and she wasn't sure that I was up to the job, so she gave the board the power to vote me out."

"What happens if they do that?"

"I become a figurehead. Of course, I still collect a salary and a healthy share of the profits, but I'll have no decision-making power." She turned to face him. "I don't intend to let that happen."

"So Richard pushed to marry you while you were still at the helm of Sheridan Trust."

"Are you insinuating—"

"I'm merely theorizing. If he did have a motive for marrying you quick, it makes it much less likely that he's dumping you. Maybe something else is going on here."

"I know there is. Sometimes, I get a feeling about things." Pausing, she studied him for a moment. "Promise you won't laugh."

"I promise."

"I get a sort of premonition when something terrible is wrong. It's a tingling sensation in my fingers."

Nick nodded. "Like the witches in *Macbeth*? 'By the pricking of my thumbs. Something wicked this way comes.' That kind of thing?"

"You promised not to laugh."

Nick raised both hands, palms out. "Hey, I'm with

you on this one. My thumbs prick every time something bad is about to go down.''

She couldn't see any trace of laughter in his eyes. ''My fingers have been tingling ever since I first read that ad. I'm sure that Richard is in some kind of trouble.''

Turning, Nick rested his arms on the railing. ''Okay. Let's shelve the runaway bridegroom theory and go with yours. He's in trouble, so he goes into hiding. He wants to communicate with you in a way that can't be traced. So he takes out the ad and makes sure it gets to you. 'Sorry I'll miss the wedding. I'll be in touch. Remember Scarlet and Annie.' So the trouble's bad enough that he can't make it to the wedding. And he's going to contact you again. Is there any particular reason he used the names Scarlet and Annie?''

''What do you mean?''

''Well, there are a lot of other things he could have said to let you know that the message could only have come from him. Why single out Scarlet and Annie?''

Tyler thought for a moment. ''Of course. They're the *tomorrow* girls. We talked about that once. Scarlet's last words are 'Tomorrow is another day,' and Annie sings 'Tomorrow'! They both believe that things just have to get better. He's telling me not to give up hope!''

''Perhaps he's being even more specific than that,'' Nick said. ''Maybe he's going to get in touch with you tomorrow—which is really *today* since you got the message yesterday.''

Laying a hand on his arm, she said, ''You really are good.''

It wasn't until she touched him that he realized how close they were. Their bodies were nearly brushing. They would if he stepped away from the railing. Then all he would have to do was put his arms around her, and he would know exactly how her body fit against his. He'd been curious about that ever since she'd walked into his office. But the curiosity was changing to something more urgent.

If he took her into his arms, he could kiss her, too. Her lips were parted, moist, waiting. A stolen kiss in Central Park—what could be the harm in that? Still, he didn't move. Oh, he could tell himself that the flush he saw in her cheeks, the excitement in her eyes was for another man, but that wasn't what was stopping him. It was something within him that made him hesitate.

Caution. The word wasn't foreign to him, but caution certainly wasn't something he prided himself on. In fact, he'd never known himself to exercise it unless the stakes were very high. A bit shaken at the realization, Nick glanced down to where her hand still rested on his arm. When he met her eyes, he managed a smile. "I think you're violating the personal space rule."

Tyler snatched her hand away as if it had been burned. "I—I apologize."

"No problem. I enjoyed it. And this way I figure I've got one personal space violation coming."

Tyler opened her mouth to reply, when suddenly a ball grazed her shoulder, then bounced away. "Who—?"

The clapping and barking noises had her whirling around. She'd forgotten all about the seal. He didn't have his ball anymore.

"He wants to play a little catch," Nick said as he moved down the path to retrieve the ball. Tyler drew in a deep breath and decided that she was grateful for the interruption. Because she wasn't sure what she would have replied to Nick's comment.

It wasn't often that someone left her nonplussed, but Nick Romano had a real knack for doing it. For a moment there, she could have sworn that he was going to kiss her. But he hadn't. And she certainly hadn't wanted him to, because it would have been a mistake. It was relief she was feeling. Tyler frowned. Why did she even feel the need to tell herself that? She watched him pick up the ball, then turn back to her. He was the most...

Once more she found herself searching for a word to describe Nick Romano. If she could just pigeonhole him, she could handle him. The clapping and barking behind her made her turn around again. The seal had climbed onto a rock that was catching a steady spray from the fountain. He barked twice, then clapped his fins together.

"He wants his ball back," Nick said, handing it to her.

Taking careful aim, Tyler tossed it in a high arc, then laughed delightedly when the seal waddled back a little, bounced it off its nose once, then twice before he had it balanced. It was her turn to clap. "Clever," she said.

"Very. He's got the best spot in the park right under that cool spray. I'm tempted to join him."

Something in his tone made her glance quickly up at him. "You're joking."

Nick shrugged. "Maybe. Maybe not. If I did, would you join me?"

She glanced quickly around. "No. I can't. You can't, either. You could get arrested."

"Probably. But I have a few friends on the force. Haven't you ever done something on impulse, just for the fun of it, consequences be damned?"

"No. Well, almost. Once."

Nick smiled. "What?"

"It was...nothing."

"Tell me."

"Shortly before I graduated from school in Switzerland, I was in Rome with two of my friends. Our parents weren't going to make it to the graduation ceremony and so we were having our own celebration. They wanted to go wading in the Trevi Fountain. So did I, but I didn't. I knew if I got caught..."

"Your grandmother would lecture you?"

"I wasn't so much worried about the lecture. I just didn't want to disappoint her."

"You should have gone wading in that fountain," Nick said. "If you want to make up for it, I'll give you a boost over this guardrail."

Smiling, Tyler shook her head. "It turned out for the best. When my two friends were arrested, I was able to follow them down to the station and pay the fine to get them out."

Nick studied her for a moment. "Always responsible. That's got to be a drag."

"No. Not—"

The ringing of the cell phone cut her off.

"I'd better answer it," she said. "It could be Richard."

Nick handed her the phone, then watched as the tension came back to her shoulders.

"Yes?" Glancing at Nick, she shook her head. "Yes, Howard, Richard is with me, and no, I can't put him on the phone...because...because he's busy right now." Two men on in-line skates roared by. "He's in-line skating, and I can't possibly run fast enough to catch him." Stepping away from the guardrail, she began to pace. "We're in Central Park. *Today?*" She stopped short and spun to face Nick. "The board of trustees want to meet later this afternoon? What on earth for?"

Moving forward, Nick covered the phone with his hand. "What's up?"

"He wants me to fly back to Boston so the board of trustees can meet."

"Tell him you can't get away. You have an in-line skating lesson scheduled."

Tyler's eyes widened. "He'll never buy that."

"Then make up a lie he will believe," Nick said.

Taking a deep breath, Tyler spoke into the phone. "Howard, I can't make a meeting today. I ran into Hamilton Bradshaw. He was at the Plaza for lunch, and I promised Richard and I would meet him for a drink later." The minute the lie was out, she saw a smile of approval on Nick's face. "Yes, I think they'll understand. And no, I can't promise that Richard will get back to you later. The whole idea of playing hooky is that you don't have to get back to people."

Closing the phone, she handed it back to Nick.

"Who's Howard?"

"He's my mother's latest husband, number four, the only one my grandmother felt was capable of handling a job at Sheridan Trust. He's been in my camp since she died."

"But you don't trust him enough to let him know the truth about Richard."

She shook her head. "It's best if I don't trust anyone with that until we know what the truth is. But I won't be able to put him off much longer."

"Maybe you won't have to. C'mon, let's walk." As he led the way down the path, he said, "This probation thing has you tied up in knots, doesn't it."

"I can handle it."

"But you can't even go in-line skating."

His tone had her smiling. "I don't know how. Besides, don't you think that's the least of my problems?"

"Maybe. But it's still a shame. They've really got you dancing to their tune. This bridegroom of yours—I'll bet your grandmother handpicked him." As soon as he spoke, he saw her stiffen.

"I think she would have liked him."

Nick glanced at her in surprise. "She never met him? How long have you known him?"

"Four months this week."

"And you met when he answered your ad in the Personals."

"No. I never did go out with any of the men who answered the ad. Richard and I met through an Internet dating service."

Nick stared at her. "Tell me you're joking."

"It was a perfectly legitimate—"

"Do you have any idea how many psychos there are out there using computers?" he asked. "What ever possessed you to be so stupid?"

Her chin shot up as she glared at him. "Stupid? Maybe if you listened instead of jumping to conclusions, Sherlock. I didn't say I met him in a chat room. I went through a very legitimate on-line dating service. Personal Connections. They responded to the ad I placed in *Attitudes*. Once I read their brochure and investigated what they could offer, I decided to use them, instead."

"Are they connected to the magazine?"

"No. But they respond to personal ads in a lot of magazines and newspapers as part of their marketing campaign. I had the security people at Sheridan Trust check it out, and I had them check Richard out, too."

"And you can bet he did the same to you. Is that when he told you that his favorite movie was *Gone with the Wind*? After he found out you were Tyler Sheridan?"

"No!" She moved closer until they were standing toe to toe. "He had no way of knowing who I was. Personal Connections guarantees complete anonymity. It was Richard who insisted on giving me his full name the first time I e-mailed him. He also insisted that I have him checked out. And he never asked who I was."

Rolling his eyes, Nick said, "How long do you think your anonymity lasted? Once I had an e-mail from you, I could trace you in a few hours at the most."

"He couldn't have traced me that way. Personal Connections relayed all my e-mails for me. He could only have traced them back to the dating service. And I'm not stupid!" She poked him in the chest. "Take it back or I'll—"

"Way to go, gal!"

Tyler whirled to face the speaker and found to her horror that a small crowd had gathered. An older woman sitting on a nearby park bench called, "You tell him!"

The man next to her laughed, while a mother urged her toddler and two teens down an adjacent path. All four were craning their necks to keep her in view.

"Show's over, folks," Nick said, taking her hand and hurrying her away across the grass.

She had to almost run to keep up with him, but she didn't complain. Only when she was sure that they could no longer be seen or heard by their audience did she speak. "I never do that."

"What? Lose your temper?"

"No. Make a scene in public."

Nick smiled at her as he slowed his pace. Her cheeks were flushed and some of her hair had fallen loose. He very much wanted to run his hands through it. "You should do it more often."

"No. Sheridans never—"

"Have any fun," he finished for her, nudging her down onto a bench.

"We do, too," she said, the anger bubbling up fresh in her.

Nick barely managed to control a laugh. Instead, he tapped his chin. "Go ahead. Take a swing. We're all alone."

She curled her hands into fists, but she kept them in her lap and frowned at him, instead. "You...stir me up."

He reached over to tuck a strand of hair behind her ear, then let his fingers trace lightly along the curve of her jaw. It was a mistake, but hell, he'd made them before.

"Don't—"

"I've got one of those personal space violations coming, remember?" Beneath his thumb, he felt her pulse jolt and then begin to race. "The problem is that you stir me up, too."

"It's just chemistry," Tyler said.

"You got that right. The question is, what are we going to do about it?"

"I don't...we can't."

"Normally, I'd be very tempted to just concentrate on the now. But I know you're big on plans, and it's always good to have as much information as possible before you make one. So let's just see what we're up against, sugar." He knew how to move quickly, so when he felt her stiffen, he settled his hand at the back of her neck.

Then, keeping his eyes on hers, he brushed his lips over hers once, twice, then moistened them carefully with his tongue. Drawing back slightly, he felt her breath mingle with his as her lashes fluttered. The need within him grew sharper as he nipped along her jaw, then lingered to taste the soft, secret spot behind her ear.

She shouldn't be doing this. The thought drummed through her mind like a chant, but she suddenly lost track of the words making it up. His mouth was impossibly soft when it returned to hers. His taste so different, so sweet. Gripping his shoulders tightly, she pulled him closer and nipped at his lips, then sighed as their honeyed warmth poured through her. It was melting her. Oh, she really shouldn't be doing this. But she wanted to. In some part of her mind that could still function, she was dimly aware that she was losing parts of herself, parts that she'd taken years to carefully build up. Drawing him closer, she used her teeth and tongue to deepen the kiss. She heard his moan, felt his heart speed up against hers. The need filled her so quickly, fully.

Her mouth was so avid, so greedy. Whatever he'd expected, whatever he'd fantasized about, Nick found it had little to do with what he was experiencing. One taste—that's what he'd promised himself. Now he wondered if he'd ever have enough. She was softer than he'd thought, incredibly so. Her hair was like warm silk against his skin as he ran his hands into it, scattering the pins. And she was anything but cool. He'd seen the temper, had known there'd be passion, but he'd never anticipated this incredible heat that radiated from her to him and back again. Dragging her closer, he suddenly changed the angle of this kiss and plunged them both closer to the fire.

This was so different. He'd never before felt the dizzying sensation that was spiraling through him, draining his control. Nor had he ever known the edgy hunger that was building within him. He had to have more. He might never get enough. The thought burned through him even as a warning bell clanged loudly in his mind. Greedily, he ignored it and took them both deeper. But it continued to ring.

The cell phone. The realization hit him like a spray of ice water and he drew back quickly. What was he doing? He'd forgotten where they were and he'd damn near pulled her to the ground in the middle of Central Park. As the phone rang again, he thrust it into her hand. "You'd better answer it."

For a moment she simply stared down at it.

"Answer it, Tyler."

Lifting it, she said, "Yes?" After a moment, she held it out to him. "Sam."

Two words, she thought as she watched him talk to his cousin. Her head was still reeling so she hadn't been sure she could get them out, but she must have. She hadn't known a kiss could do that. Fill you and drain you so completely at the same time. There was only one thing she was sure of. She couldn't possibly let it happen again. But how in the world, now that she'd experienced it, was she supposed to forget it?

"So much for your faith in Personal Connections," Nick said as he snapped the phone shut and jammed it into his pocket.

Tyler frowned. "What are you talking about?"

"Sam just learned that your bridegroom is a fake."

3

FAKE. Even as the word spun through her mind, Tyler said, "Richard is most certainly not a fake."

"Richard James Lawrence was the third son born to Anita and Robert Lawrence of Louisville, Kentucky, and he died in an auto accident twelve years ago."

"That's impossible." Even as she spoke, an image had slipped into her mind: she was standing at the altar alone, her dress flowing around her. Fear twisted in her stomach.

"The numbers don't lie," Nick said. "Sam traced him back to his birthplace using the social security number you gave. Whoever this guy is that Personal Connections hooked you up with, he's not the Richard James Lawrence who belongs to that social security number."

Her fingers were tingling again. Curling them into fists, Tyler fought off a wave of panic. It couldn't be true. *Think!* "Then who is the Richard James Lawrence who's been working as an accountant for Cramer, Brooks and Stapleton for the past six years?"

"Whoever he is, the scam he's been running is about to come crashing down around his ears," Nick vowed.

When he started to rise from the bench, Tyler grabbed his arm and pulled him back. "I had Richard checked out. If he was dead, Sheridan's security people would have found it out."

"Not if they didn't check back far enough."

"Well, my roommate from college can tell you he's real. She took a course with Richard at Columbia just two years ago."

"Is that the same roommate who dared you to run an ad in the Personals?"

"Yes."

"I want to talk to her," Nick said.

"Fine. She has an office on Wall Street."

IN SPITE OF THE air-conditioning, the inside of the taxi seemed stuffy and warm. And silent. Tyler was grateful for that. She needed a moment to focus. To think of some explanation for what Nick had discovered about Richard.

There had to be one. But she couldn't for the life of her figure out what it could be. Because the man sitting only a foot or so away from her was distracting her. That kiss they'd just shared...the heat that had flowed through her, the wanting that it had left in its wake— *No*, she wasn't going to let herself think about it now. She had to concentrate on Richard, the man she'd agreed to marry in eight days. Closing her eyes, she drew in a deep breath and tried to center herself. In a moment, the weakness would pass. She'd worked hard to develop willpower and control, and it would serve her now.

The driver leaned on the horn as he aimed the taxi suddenly into the left lane. When he slammed on the brakes, Tyler made a quick grab for the handle, but she wasn't in time to keep herself from sliding against Nick. She planted both hands against his chest just as he gripped her arms, and they were in the same position they'd been in when he'd kissed her in the park. Her response was immediate; she felt the heat pour through her, along with the knowledge. All either one of them had to do was close the small distance, and it would happen again. That sharp bright whip of desire, the dazzling spiral of pleasure. She knew now what was waiting for her. And she felt the pull, strong and steady, to move forward, just a little, and take—

"No," she said as she made herself draw back. "I can't... I won't."

"You already did, once," Nick said as he leaned back against the door. If he could have managed to get farther away, he would have. Because for a moment there, he hadn't wanted to take no for an answer. And he'd always been able to before. It was more evidence for his theory that Tyler Sheridan was different for him. And that made her dangerous.

"Kissing you was a mistake. I won't make it again."

He studied her for a moment. Her hair was still mussed from his hands, her cheeks were flushed, and the pulse at her throat was beating fast. She had to be thinking of what they'd shared, what they could share again, just as he was. "You're wrong. We're both going to make that particular mistake again."

"No." She shook her head. "You said it yourself. It's just chemistry."

"But it could be passion."

"There's a difference?"

"Chemistry burns out quickly. True passion just grows more intense with each indulgence. Of course, we'd have to experiment a little, find out exactly what it is between us."

Tyler stared at him. Did the man ever take anything seriously? But beneath the teasing light in his eyes, she could see something else, something that reached out to her. And she could feel deep within herself the desire to reach out to him, too. It was something she'd struggled all her life against. *Something she'd wished all her life for?* No, that couldn't be true. She wouldn't let it be true. "Passion or chemistry. I don't care to indulge. It can't, and it won't, lead anywhere for either one of us."

"I'm not sure all the facts are in on that."

Chin lifted, Tyler met his eyes squarely. "I don't intend to investigate it any further. I've seen where passion leads, and I promised myself that I would never travel down that path."

It was the bleak look in her eyes that kept him from reaching out to her, pulling her close and proving her wrong. There was a secret there, and he vowed he'd learn it. But he could wait.

"So your relationship with this bridegroom of yours is devoid of passion?"

"That's not what I said."

Nick's brows rose. "It's certainly what you implied."

"It's true that I didn't want my relationship with Richard—or with any man—to be based merely on passion. That's why I decided to use Personal Connections, so that I could make sure before we ever met in person that Richard—or whoever he is—and I were compatible on more important levels."

"Ah," Nick said.

The look she shot him was pure ice. "What's that supposed to mean?"

Grinning, Nick shrugged. "Just 'ah.' We detectives say it a lot. It's our most frequently used expression after 'aha!'"

"This the place?" the driver asked as he rammed the taxi into the curb.

Tyler glanced out the window. "Yes." Raising a hand to automatically smooth her hair, she suddenly remembered that it was down, and that the pins were scattered somewhere on a path in Central Park. "Wait. I can't go in there looking like this."

"You look fine to me."

"I look like a ragamuffin." Unsnapping her purse, she drew out a brush.

"Here, let me," Nick said, taking it from her. "Turn around."

"No, I can—"

"It'll save time. You can check your makeup while I take care of this."

For one second, Tyler weighed her options. Wrestling with Nick Romano for her hairbrush or giving in and preserving her dignity. She did what a true Sheridan would do and turned to dig in her purse for her compact.

"I've got two younger sisters," Nick said as he drew the brush through her hair. "For years my mom and I had to get them ready for church on Sunday...."

Whatever he was saying had become an unrecognizable buzz of sound in Tyler's ears. It had been a mistake to allow him to touch her. And she'd only made it worse by opening her compact. Because now she could see as well as feel his hands on her. She discovered it was incredibly erotic to watch his fingers move from where they rested lightly on her shoulder to draw her hair back over her ear, then brush across the nape of her neck. The flames started there, then fanned out quickly until her blood turned thick and warm. An image filled her mind of those fingers stroking softly, surely, all over her body. Her nerve endings began to throb with just the thought of it, and it was all she could do not to lean back against him. She wasn't aware of letting the compact slip through her fingers, only of the sudden weight when it landed on her lap.

"You two done back there?" the driver asked, twisting in his seat. "I got another fare waving at me on the corner."

Tyler snatched up her compact, shoved it into her purse and pushed open the door of the taxi. Only by summoning up all her control did she prevent herself from running into the lobby of the glass-and-steel building. Instead, she pushed through the revolving door, then cut a neat path through the crowd of conservatively dressed men and women milling around her, while she tried to gather her thoughts.

She had to do something about Nick Romano and his effect on her, and she had to do it now before things went any farther. When he caught up with her, she drew in a deep breath, then turned to face him.

"Before we go up to see Stevie, we should talk," she said.

"Great minds think alike." Nick drew her out of the traffic pattern toward the wall.

"We are not going to kiss again."

His brows rose, but he said nothing in reply.

"Well?" she prodded.

"I don't like to lie unless I absolutely have to. If we're going to continue to spend time together, I'm going to want to kiss you, and you're going to want to kiss me back. Tell me I'm wrong."

"I... We don't have to do it just because we want to. We're adults. And I'm about to be married."

"To a man who isn't who he claims to be and who also seems to be missing."

"Richard may have a very good explanation for everything when we find him. Which is a very good reason why we shouldn't kiss again. We have to concentrate on finding him. And kissing you...it's...distracting.''

"Oh, it's that all right, sugar.''

Tyler studied him for a moment. He was smiling at her as if he didn't have a care in the world. And for some reason she couldn't understand, she wanted to smile right back at him. She bit down hard on the side of her cheek until the urge passed. "It's also impossible. Even if I weren't getting married to Richard, even if I were free, I just don't want what seems to be happening between us. I...we just don't have anything in common. We come from different worlds, and I'm not interested in a relationship that's based on just chemistry. Or passion.''

The smile faded from his face. She should have been pleased that she'd wiped it off, but the hot flash of anger she saw in his eyes made her take one quick step back against the wall.

"You hit the nail right on the head, sugar. We do come from different worlds. And while we're at it, we might as well get it all out. I want you. I'm not sure I like it any more than you do. But I'm also pretty sure that's not going to stop what's going to happen between us. Maybe you ought to take the first piece of advice I gave you and hire a different PI.''

She knew he was right. It would be the wisest choice. But some instinct deep inside told her that he was her best bet in finding Richard. And she had to make that her first priority. Besides, Sheridans didn't run. She shook her head. "No. I trust you. I need you to help me find Richard. All we have to do is lay some ground rules.''

"I'm better at breaking them than keeping them.''

Tyler prayed for patience. "One rule, then. We'll keep it simple. I just want your word that you won't kiss me again."

He studied her for a moment. "I'll promise that I won't initiate a kiss."

Tyler narrowed her gaze. "There's a *but* in there."

Nick grinned. "You're sharp, Sheridan. I can see why you're successful in the boardroom. Here's the deal. I won't initiate any kisses. *But* if you kiss me, I'll kiss you right back. Think you can keep yourself under control?"

Her chin lifted. "Of course, I can."

"Then let's go. I want to talk to your college roommate."

As Tyler followed him to the elevators, she wondered if she was ever going to feel certain she'd made her point with this man.

HANOVER SECURITIES occupied the entire fortieth floor of the building, and Stevie Hanover's office was tucked into a corner with windows on two sides offering a view of Central Park. That didn't surprise Nick, since Tyler had informed him that Stevie was planning on running her father's company one day.

What did surprise him was Stevie Hanover herself. She wore her red hair cut short in an almost military style. That along with the short skirt and the stylish boots laced up to her knees gave her a one-of-a-kind look on Wall Street.

The contrast between the two women was sharp. If Tyler had taken pains all her life to fit into the mold of the successful investment advisor, it was clear that Stevie had put just as much effort into breaking out of it. But the moment she sprang up off the edge of her desk and enveloped Tyler in a warm hug, Nick decided he liked her.

"Tyler! If you'd let me know you were coming, I'd have cleared my—" She broke off the moment she drew back and looked at her friend. "What's wrong?"

"I...it's..."

"Sit down." Nudging Tyler gently into a chair, Stevie grabbed a box of tissues off her desk and pulled several out. "Here—"

"I—" Tyler dabbed at her eyes "—I'm not crying."

"Of course, you're not," Stevie said. "Sheridans never cry." Then she turned to give Nick a quick, thorough look, up and then down. "Are you the reason she's upset?"

Her tone was quiet enough, but Nick found himself grateful when Tyler came to his defense.

"No," Tyler said as she balled the tissues in her hand. "He's Nick Romano, a private investigator who's helping me. Richard is...missing."

Stevie stared at her friend. "Missing? Tell me."

When Tyler had finished giving her a quick rundown, Stevie glanced at Nick. "When you find him, I'm going to kill him." Then she turned back to Tyler. "What is he thinking of? The wedding is a week from tomorrow!"

"I know."

Squatting, Stevie grasped Tyler's hands firmly. "What can I do?"

"You can answer Nick's questions."

Stevie shifted her attention back to Nick. "Ask away."

"Tyler said you were the one who encouraged her to place a personal ad in *Attitudes Magazine.*"

"I dared her to do it. I also encouraged her to use Personal Connections when she got the brochure. She was becoming a hermit."

"Tyler said you knew Richard Lawrence before she met him. You took a course with him two years ago."

Stevie nodded. "A tax course. They offer them every time the government fiddles around with the tax code."

"What can you tell me about him?"

"Not much. He seemed a nice enough guy. I told Tyler all this when she first started dating him."

"Did you ever date him?"

"No." Stevie glanced at Tyler. "I might have, but at the time I had sworn off business types. I was into musicians. I did meet with him several times. A few of us would get together before class, share notes, and hit the caffeine so that we could keep awake for the lecture."

"Did he ever mention anything about his background?"

"I know he worked at Cramer, Brooks and Stapleton. I took his card, and I referred a couple of clients to him."

"And they were pleased?" Nick asked.

"I never received any complaints."

"He ever mention his family?"

"Not that I can recall." Stevie frowned as she looked from Nick to Tyler. "How long has he been missing?"

"Since yesterday, as far as I can tell," Tyler began. As she continued to fill her friend in on the details, Nick found his mind returning to what had happened in the lobby. He'd given her the option of going to Sam, of ending whatever it was that was happening between them before it started. But as he watched her talking to her friend, he wasn't altogether sure that he would have let her go. Because it had been right then, when she'd refused, that the pricking in his thumbs had begun. It hadn't stopped yet, and Nick was almost sure it had more to do with the woman than the case.

When Tyler finished, Stevie turned to Nick. "So there are two Richard James Lawrences?"

"So it seems. Someone with Richard's social security number died twelve years ago," explained Nick. "And someone still using that same social security number has been working at Cramer, Brooks and Stapleton. You never noticed anything odd about him?"

"No." A faint frown appeared on her forehead. "Just..."

"What?" Nick prodded.

"When Tyler first told me about him, I remember thinking it was odd that he was using a dating service. He didn't strike me as the kind of guy who'd have trouble attracting women."

"But you didn't think it was odd that Tyler was using one. In fact you said you encouraged it."

Stevie's brows lifted. "When someone isn't dating at all, drastic measures are called for. In fact, when she told me that she'd met Richard through them, I thought I'd give them a shot myself. I even filled out one of their questionnaires."

"Do you still have it?" asked Nick.

"Yes. I downloaded it." Moving to a nearby cabinet, she opened a drawer. "By the time I'd finished all the paperwork, I'd changed my mind. I thought I'd already met Mr. Right on my own. Here it is." As she handed a stapled set of papers to Nick, she said, "You think Richard's after her money?"

"Maybe," Nick said. "But it's a strange time to disappear. He doesn't have the money yet. And he's evidently been masquerading successfully as Richard

Lawrence for some time. Could be his past has caught up with him."

"Which means he really could be in trouble," Tyler said. "That's what I've been telling you from the very beginning." She held out her hands. "That's why my fingers have been tingling."

"So THAT'S YOUR college roommate," Nick said, once they had stepped out onto the street. "The two of you certainly don't seem to have rubbed off on one another."

Tyler smiled. "A lot of people have that reaction. Stevie goes for shock effect."

"And you've never been tempted to do that?"

"Yes. Once I nearly got a tattoo. Stevie asked me to go with her, and while she was getting hers, I looked at the pictures on the wall. I even picked one out."

She'd lowered her voice. Nick wondered if she was aware of it. "Which one?" he asked.

"Pegasus."

"The flying horse. Good choice. Why didn't you go for it?"

She shrugged. "I thought of what my grandmother would say. Or some of the board members—if they ever found out. I just don't have Stevie's guts."

"Bet she's not on probation in her job," he remarked as he took her arm and urged her toward the corner.

"No. And she's good at it. She's specializing in bringing Generation X on board as regular investors at Hanover Security. It's a challenge to attract them because most of them think they can handle their own portfolios by day trading off their laptops."

"You could do that for Sheridan Trust, too, couldn't you?"

"I'm planning on it. Bringing Bradshaw Enterprises on board is step one of my plan. Hamilton Bradshaw's built a reputation for investing in young entrepreneurs, and he's attracted to Sheridan Trust because he believes in family-run companies. He was very pleased when I announced my engagement. Before that, he was a little nervous dealing with a young, single woman. If I don't get married next Saturday, he might have second thoughts."

"Well, he shouldn't. Whether or not you get married doesn't change what Sheridan Trust can offer him."

"Right." Pausing, Tyler looked around as Nick led her into a coffee shop. "What are we doing?"

"Coffee-break time," he said as he settled her in a booth. "Detectives need them quite regularly, especially after an all-night tailing job."

Tyler glanced at her watch. "Isn't there something else we should be doing?"

"We are. Stevie just gave us more information, and we need to let it roll around awhile until something surfaces."

"It doesn't seem to me she told us anything we don't already know," Tyler said.

"That's because you're not the detective, and I am. How about a tall iced cappuccino?"

"No thanks. I don't drink caffeine."

Nick stared at her. "You're kidding. How can you survive?"

"Quite easily."

He made a face. "Don't tell me you prefer one of those herbal teas that smell like dried grass?"

"Orange juice, please," Tyler said to a hovering waitress.

"Make mine a double iced cappuccino," Nick said, then turned to find Tyler frowning at him.

"You know, in addition to the fact that it's addictive, coffee is one of the worst possible things you can drink during a heat wave. It dehydrates you," she said.

"A small price to pay for that wonderful jolt it gives your system."

"In exchange for the 'jolt,' I don't have mood swings, and I sleep better at night."

Nick shook his head. "That sounds awfully dull to me. I'll opt for mood swings. And at night, well, a good night's sleep ranks really low on my list. What's your position on chocolate? That contains caffeine."

His gaze was so intent, the concern in his eyes so real, Tyler found herself confessing. "When it comes to chocolate, I cheat."

"Thank heavens."

She couldn't prevent a laugh at the relief she heard in his voice. "Richard never cheated. I could never have confessed my weakness to him."

Nick's gaze narrowed. "You're telling me he was anti-caffeine, too?"

"Oh, yes."

"That's odd."

"What is?"

"Didn't Stevie say that she used to meet him and a few others so they could load up on caffeine before class? Maybe his anti-caffeine phase only began recently."

Tyler shook her head. "He told me that he gave it up after his last all-nighter in college. He was very proud of the fact that he'd never fallen off the wagon, not even during tax season."

While the waitress served their drinks, Nick pulled

the Personal Connections questionnaire out of his pocket and flipped through it. "There's a whole section here on food and drink preferences, and one on movies, books, plays, sports." He paused to look up at her. "Did you ever actually see Richard's questionnaire?"

"No. I never saw mine again once I filled it out and mailed it in. They feed the information into their computer and run matches with their client base."

"What happens then?"

"When they got the results, they called me up and told me they had what they were predicting would be a perfect match."

"I bet," Nick said.

Tyler studied him for a moment. "You don't think much of dating services, do you."

He folded the questionnaire and returned it to his pocket. "Let's just say that I don't think that a 'personal connection' between two people can be predicted by matching up a bunch of answers to questions."

"And just what do you think *can* predict that kind of connection?"

"Passion, for one thing. If a relationship doesn't have that, it doesn't matter if you like the same movies or musicals or sports teams. With it, it doesn't matter if you come from different worlds or different planets. Or—" he raised his iced cappuccino in a toast "—whether or not you are pro- or anti-caffeine."

Tyler tried to ignore the shiver that ran up her spine. When he spoke of passion, when he looked at her in that intent way, she could almost believe that her grandmother had been right all along. What if she really *was* her mother's daughter? Quickly she pushed the thought aside. "Passion can die, and then what are you left with? After my father died, I watched my mother get carried away by her so-called passion for one man after another, and it never lasted. I don't intend to follow in her footsteps."

"So you went to Personal Connections in search of a strictly platonic relationship?"

"Yes, I wanted it to start off that way, and Richard and I matched at above the eighty-five percent level. They told me it was one of the best connections they'd ever seen."

Nick took a long drink of his cappuccino. "And you think you're the only client they told that to?"

"I know for a fact that they didn't say that to everybody. They gave me telephone numbers of some of their previous clients. Some were more satisfied than others. None of them claimed that they matched at such a high level."

"Interesting. Did they call Richard with the same information about the eighty-five percent match?"

"Yes. But it was up to us whether or not we wanted to give out our e-mail addresses. And they only release that information if both parties agree to it."

Nick stirred what remained in the bottom of his glass while he thought a bit. "Your friend Stevie thought it was odd that Richard was using a dating service. Didn't you?"

"I asked him why the first time I e-mailed him, and he said that he wanted to find someone he shared a lot of interests with because he was tired of relationships that would burn hot for a while and then fizzle."

"So, once again, he revealed himself to be in perfect sync with you."

For a moment Tyler didn't speak, as with one finger she traced a path through the frost on her glass. "You're thinking that the match-up was too perfect."

"Bingo."

Tyler thought for a moment. "What if I told you that Richard's favorite baseball team was the Red Sox?"

"I'd say he's either in need of immediate psychiatric care in a long-term facility, or the match-up was rigged. C'mon."

"Where are we going?" Tyler asked, as he dropped a bill on the table and led the way out of the coffee shop.

"I'm taking you back to your hotel. It's time I did a little detecting."

"Absolutely not," Tyler said as she followed him out onto the sidewalk. "According to your theory, Richard—"

"Richard is probably not his real name."

"Right. According to your theory, not only is my bridegroom a fake, but he's a liar. And if you think I'm going to sit quietly in my hotel room while you—"

Nick's sharp whistle cut off what she was going to say and brought a taxi veering to the curb. As he reached for the door, Tyler grabbed his arm. "Are you listening to me?"

"There you go violating my personal space again," Nick pointed out. As she fisted her hand, he grinned. "You know you're cute when you get mad."

"*Cute?* I'll give you—"

"We better discuss it in the taxi. Unless you want to make another scene in public."

As THE TAXI JOLTED to a stop in front of the Plaza, Tyler pushed open the door and climbed out. "Call me when you're done," she bit out without looking back. The one thing she couldn't do was fault Nick Romano's logic. She couldn't afford to be caught breaking and entering Richard's office, and that was what Nick intended to

do. Of course, it might go smoothly, but if it didn't...
He'd painted a very vivid picture of being hauled into a
precinct for questioning. She couldn't take the chance.

But oh, how she wanted to, she thought as she
glanced back at the taxi. Even now, she wanted to insist
he take her with him. The struggle within her was one
she'd waged all her life. Someday she was going to
make a list of all the things she'd wanted to do, but
hadn't been able to, she thought as she turned back toward the hotel. And then what would she do? Burn it
probably. She wondered if being Tyler Sheridan would
ever get easier.

She was three steps from the revolving door to the
lobby when someone gripped her elbow.

"What are you—?" She turned, jerking her arm, but
the man's grip held firm. He was medium height, sol-
idly built, and she'd never seen him before in her life.

"Richard sent me," he said, urging her away from the
door.

"Where is he?" Tyler said, trying to stop their progress toward a van parked ahead at the curb.

"I'm taking you there—" the man said.

"I don't think so," Nick said, bringing the side of his
hand down hard on the man's arm and breaking his
grip on Tyler. "Get into the lobby, Tyler," he said as he
slammed his fist into the man's face.

She'd backed up one step when she saw another man
climb out of the van. She grabbed Nick's arm. "There're
two of them."

"Damn it, I told you to—" Nick was cut off as the first
man barreled into him headfirst and sent him flying
into Tyler. She cushioned his fall as they both landed on
the sidewalk. By the time he scrambled to his feet, the
two goons had made it into the van, and it was peeling

away from the curb. Turning, he held his hand out to Tyler. "Friends of yours?"

"They were going to take me to Richard," she said.

"A fake, a liar, and a kidnapper, too. That's an interesting bridegroom you picked out for yourself, sugar."

4

NICK KEPT HIS HAND TIGHT on Tyler's arm as they
crossed the hotel lobby and entered a waiting elevator.
He needed a moment, that was all. By the time they
reached Tyler's floor, he'd have the lid clamped down
tight on the fear and the anger that were still roiling
around in him. The more potent of the two was the fear
that had sliced through him when he'd seen the first
man approach her and take her arm. Even as Nick had
jumped out of the taxi and shoved a pedestrian aside to
get to her, a dozen frightening scenarios had run
through his mind. Any one of them could have been a
reality if the taxi had taken him away just a few seconds
sooner.

Ruthlessly, he pushed the images away. In his business, keeping a cool head was essential. Emotions led to
mistakes, and mistakes could be deadly. That's why he
was furious with himself. From the moment Tyler Sheridan had shown him that letter from her grandmother,
he'd been letting his feelings get the better of him. That
had been his first mistake.

Turning, he studied her profile for a moment. Her
face was perfectly composed, her eyes fixed on the
flashing digital numbers that tracked the swift ascent of
the elevator. There was no sign that she'd nearly been
snatched right out from under his nose.

She was a regular ice princess, he thought as the

doors slid open. He could admire her for it, but at the same time it annoyed the hell out of him. Releasing her arm, he followed her down the thickly carpeted hall until she stopped at her door.

"The key," he said, holding out his hand.

Slipping it from her purse, she handed it to him without a word.

"Here's the plan," he said. "I'm going to check and make sure the room's clear. You're going to back off a few steps and stay put. Any noise you hear, you're going to run away as fast as you can and use the stairs. Got it?"

At her nod, he stood to one side of the door and silently cursed the fact that he hadn't brought his gun. Another mistake. He couldn't afford a third one. Carefully, he slipped the plastic strip into the lock, then withdrew it. As soon as the green light winked, he twisted the handle and sent the door slamming into the wall. Counting to three, he stepped into the room. A river of oatmeal-colored carpeting ran down a corridor, then flowed to a wall of windows that framed a line of skyscrapers in the distance. The sitting area was empty. Sliding through an open doorway, he checked the bedroom and the closet. One glance into the mirror-walled bathroom told him there was no one lurking in there, either.

Then he turned his attention back to the bedroom. "Damn it!"

"Disappointed that you didn't find anyone hiding under the bed?"

Whirling, he saw Tyler standing in the doorway. "No. I'm just cursing the fact that the maid's already cleaned the room."

"They tend to do that in first-class hotels."

For the first time since he'd jumped out of the cab, Nick felt some of his tension ease. "Yeah, but it wreaks havoc with clues."

Tyler's glanced around with a frown. "You think they came up here?"

He shrugged, but chose his words carefully. "They might have taken the opportunity to browse around while they were waiting to pick you up."

"This hotel has a very good security system."

"This hotel also has employees who might not be immune to a bribe. You can check to make sure that nothing's missing while you pack."

"Pack?"

"You can't stay here. It's not safe."

"I'm not leaving. Richard knows I stay at the Plaza whenever I come to town. He may try to get in touch with me here."

Nick wanted to swear again. She had a point. Ruthlessly, he shoved his feelings aside. "Pack anyway. My friend Harry Putnam heads up security here. I'll have him move you to one of their limited-access suites."

He saw her take a deep breath, open her mouth and then shut it. Whatever it was she really wanted to say to him wasn't going to get out. He couldn't help but admire her control.

"All right. I'll pack, but before we leave here, we're coming up with a plan."

He wasn't about to argue. Yet. Leaning against the wall, he watched her take a suit out of the closet. The style was an almost perfect match for the one she was wearing.

"Don't you ever wear anything but those neat little suits?" he asked.

"Of course," she said, glancing at him.

"When?" he asked.

She frowned. "When I...when I'm not working."

Nick's brows rose. "So visiting your bridegroom for the weekend is work?"

"No, of course not," she said as she walked to the dresser and began removing lingerie. "I just feel more comfortable in suits. My grandmother never approved of wearing anything more casual to work. It would present the wrong image...."

Nick listened to her explanation with only one part of his mind. The other part was focused on the thin bits of silk and lace she was folding carefully and placing in her suitcase. It occurred to him that she probably had something similar on right now. Even as the heat shot through him and tightened into a hard knot in his center, an image filled his mind. She wore only the ivory bit of nothing she was holding. He could easily imagine what it would be like to touch her—the warmth of her skin tempting him through the cool, soft silk. He could even anticipate dampening that silk with his mouth and sampling that honeyed sweetness. Drugging and potent, the flavor would seep into him as he slowly drew the silk away and feasted on the smooth flesh beneath.

"...Richard prefers me in suits," she was saying.

It was the mention of her fiancé that made the image fade from his mind and another take its place: Richard touching that ivory silk, Richard tasting... Something sharp twisted in his gut, and he stepped quickly into the bathroom. It was a mistake. His third, he thought as her scent wrapped around him and his gaze went straight to the whirlpool tub. Another image slipped into his mind. No, he was not going to think of the two of them....

Turning around, he nearly walked right into her. "Let's go," he said, taking her arm.

"I have to get my makeup."

"Harry will take care of it," he said as he hurried her out of the bathroom. "C'mon."

"Now wait just a minute." She jerked herself free and turned to face him. "I want to know your plan first."

"I told you before. A good PI survives by living in the now."

"A good CEO always has a plan."

He grabbed both her arms this time. It was another mistake. His biggest one yet. They were close, their bodies nearly touching. He thought fleetingly of the promise he'd made not to initiate a kiss. But beneath his hands, her skin had already heated, and he could feel her pulse racing. Suddenly, only one plan formed in his mind. "How's this?" he asked as he jerked her against him and closed his mouth over hers.

He'd expected resistance. If she'd struggled at all, he might have been able to stop. Maybe. But the moment her body, slender, strong, began to melt into his, any hope he had swirled away like the last thoughts of a drowning man. When her lips parted, inviting him in, he went, and then he stopped thinking at all.

All he knew then was desire, hot, molten. Never before had it erupted this quickly. But she was so alive, her response so immediate. Everywhere he touched, it beckoned him, trapped him. He wanted her...no, he needed her now. Tearing his mouth from hers, he pressed his lips to her throat. He tried to gather his thoughts, but they wouldn't come. The realization should have frightened him, given him the strength to pull back. Instead, he dragged her closer.

Tyler hadn't known that it was possible for her mind

to just click shut. But it must have. Otherwise she would have been pulling away. She wouldn't be straining closer, and her hands wouldn't be slipping beneath his T-shirt, greedily exploring that smooth taut skin on his back. She shouldn't, she really shouldn't, be doing this. But oh, how much she wanted to. It was against the rules she'd struggled all her life to follow. In some tiny, far-off corner of her brain, she heard each rule shatter, then spin away. The freedom streamed through her. There was only now. There were only the sensations battering through her. The explosions of pleasure that only Nick could bring her. And she could feel every-thing—the hard line of his body, the heat of his lips bruising her throat, the scrape of his teeth that sent a ribbon of fire through her. And his hands. They weren't gentle as he slipped them beneath her blouse and took them on a meticulous journey from her waist, up her side and around to cup her breast. They spoke of the ur-gency of his need and inflamed her own. She arched against him, then wrapped her arms around him until she couldn't breathe, couldn't think.

He could have her now. The realization pounded through him. The bed was behind her. They could be on it, rolling across it...it would be crazy, wonderful... The images filled his mind just as completely as she filled his senses.

"Nick, please."

The sound was only a whisper in his ear. It was the only thing that brought him back to some semblance of reason. Dragging his mouth from hers, he drew in a deep breath. For a moment, he'd forgotten everything. Who he was, who she was. He'd completely lost him-self in her. No woman, nothing, had ever done that to him before. It was simply caution, not fear, that gave him the strength to set her away from him.

For a moment after he released her, all she did was stare at him. She looked every bit as stunned as he felt. But the desire, the wanting still crackled in the air between them. "Why...why did you do that?" she asked.

It was the same question he was asking himself. He said the first thing that came to mind. "Irresistible impulse."

"Irresistible impulse!"

It happened very fast. He saw the anger light her eyes at the same time he saw her fist coming. Both registered in his mind an instant before he moved, and the blow grazed his cheek. The impact was still enough to unbalance him, and the next thing he knew he was sitting on the bed, staring at her. "Why did you do *that?*"

"I'm sorry—I... You're bleeding!" Once again, she looked as stunned as he felt.

He rubbed his cheek. "It's just a scratch. You must have gotten me with your ring. I think I'll survive."

"I never do that." She stared down at her hand, at the one that was still curled into a fist. Slowly, she straightened out the fingers. She'd cut him with her engagement ring. Pulling it off, she slipped it into her pocket. "I'm sorry." She glanced up at him. "I've never punched anyone in my entire life."

"That was a good one, sugar. You knocked me off balance! Who's been giving you lessons?"

"No one. I don't... I'm not a physical person. And Sheridans never hit people. We never lose our temper. I don't know what came over me."

"Anger, frustration, fear—the same things that came over me," Nick said. Though he wanted to, he didn't reach out and touch her. "Attempted kidnappings always bring out the worst in me."

She studied him for a minute, her eyes narrowing. "And what do you do if the attempt succeeds?"

"It never does. Not on my watch, sugar."

Her lips twitched. "You're—almost insufferable."

Absurdly relieved that the lost, stunned look had finally disappeared from her eyes, Nick threw back his head and laughed. "You're not so bad yourself." Then rising from the bed, he urged her toward the door. "C'mon."

"I still want a plan," Tyler said.

"Nag, nag, nag," Nick complained. But when she stopped dead in her tracks, he said, "We're going to my apartment so I can take a quick shower and change. That will give us a chance to mull things over, and then we can make as many plans as you want."

TEN MINUTES LATER, Nick opened the door of a taxi and urged her inside. Tyler slid across the seat to the opposite door. The window was open, which meant that the air-conditioning was probably nonexistent. Ignoring the feel of her blouse sticking to her back, Tyler concentrated on the simple task of breathing. The moment they'd left the hotel through the side entrance, Nick had grabbed her hand and started to jog. He'd warned her that he planned to lose anyone who might be tailing them, but she hadn't expected the equivalent of a cross-country run. She lost track of how many streets they'd dashed down or across, until he'd finally stepped off the curb and whistled sharply for a taxi.

"Not bad at all for a CEO," he said now, after giving the cab driver an address. "It's got to be hell running in those heels."

Tyler summoned up the energy to turn and face him squarely. "You did that on purpose, didn't you. Just to test me."

He placed a hand over his heart and winced as if she'd just hit him with an arrow. "Would I do something like that? Especially to a woman with a right cross like yours?"

She didn't bother to reply. At the moment it was much more important to breathe and to catch whatever breeze was making its way in through the window. Out of the corner of her eye, she could see Nick fish her cell phone out of his pocket.

"I'm going to check in with Sam," he said.

"I'll be mulling," she managed, and had the satisfaction of seeing his lips curve as he punched in numbers.

As much as she might suspect they'd run longer and down more streets than necessary, she was absolutely certain that no one was following them. Nick Romano was good at what he did. He could certainly move when he put his mind to it. And he was efficient, too. She would have had to make a list first in order to accomplish all that he had before they'd left the hotel. First, he'd convinced his friend Harry, who headed up security, to assign a man to the desk. Any visitors, anyone delivering a message to her, would be monitored very carefully. Then he'd used Harry's fax machine to send Sam the picture of Richard that she carried in her wallet. Nick was checking with his cousin now to make sure he'd gotten it.

Leaning back against the seat, Tyler swallowed a sigh. Nothing that they'd learned so far made any sense. Who in the world was the man she thought she'd fallen in love with? In her mind, she tried to summon up a picture of him. But the neatly combed brown hair, the handsome, almost pretty features seemed blurred. Even his eyes—she'd never been able to pinpoint their color, not green and not brown. Whatever color they were, they paled in comparison to the piercing, almost black eyes of Nick Romano.

Turning, she studied the man sitting next to her. He was frowning, tapping one hand impatiently against his knee as he waited to talk to his cousin. In the six months she'd known Richard, he'd never once stirred her up or drawn the emotions out of her that Nick had. She'd known this man less than four hours, and he'd already kissed her twice.

And twice she'd...what? *Responded*. Yes, that was a nice, safe, respectable word. One she could live with, but one that couldn't even begin to describe the feelings that had pounded through her.

With very little effort, she could recall each separate sensation that had streamed through her when he'd grabbed her in her hotel room. Where his hand had pressed against her back, her spine had simply melted. And the heat—it had bubbled up hot and molten from the pit of her stomach, spreading through her veins and lapping along her nerve endings in wave after wave of liquid fire. Even more seductive was the thought that had slipped traitorously into her mind that no other man would ever make her feel this way. Ever.

She could recall so clearly the edge of the bed pressing against the back of her legs, and how much she'd wanted to be with him on that bed, to roll with him across it.... Opening her eyes, Tyler shoved the image ruthlessly out of her mind, only to find herself staring at Nick's hand where it was still resting on his knee. All she had to do was to look at it, or at the other one as it gripped the phone, to have the desire springing up in her again.

"Damn!" Nick swore as he snapped the phone shut.

Passion. She had it for her work. But she'd promised herself it would never enter any relationship she had with a man. And it never had, until now.

"Bad news?" she asked.

"Sam has to get back to me. He's on another line."

If it were a problem at Sheridan Trust, she would face it head-on. She'd follow the same rule here. "While you're waiting, there's something we have to get straight," she said. "We have to do something about what's happening between us."

Nick smiled at her. "I'd be more than happy to do something, but first you have to promise not to slug me again."

"I'm serious."

"Well, if we *have* to be serious, I owe you an apology for initiating that kiss back in the hotel room. I promised you I wouldn't, and I usually make a point of keeping my word. You're a powerful temptation to me."

The hurt that had sliced through her at his words of apology was replaced by a flood of other emotions— one was pleasure that she had that kind of power and the other was...anticipation? Before she could think of anything to say, he continued, "Under the circumstances, I can't renew my promise because I want to kiss you again right now."

Tyler felt her pulse jolt and then begin to race. The heat in the car suddenly seemed to increase by several degrees. Clearing her throat, she lifted a hand to tuck her hair back behind her ear, but Nick beat her to it, letting his fingers linger before taking her hand in his. "I want to do more than kiss you, Tyler."

"We can't," she managed.

"Speak for yourself."

She drew in a deep breath. "I can't, then. You and I...we're smart people. We come from different worlds, and we have nothing in common except..."

"Passion," Nick finished for her.

"Yes. And I told you before, I've seen what it does to people. That's not the kind of relationship I want."

"We don't always get what we want." His tone was soft, but there was no mistaking the threat in his tone, the promise in his eyes.

Tyler let out the breath she hadn't been aware she was holding and very deliberately withdrew her hand from his. "Right now, I want to find Richard. Why don't we concentrate on that?"

Nick's eyes narrowed. "Ah, yes, the missing bridegroom. And when we do find him, just what do you intend to do with him?"

"I'll know better once he has a chance to explain."

"Explain? Oh, I want to be there when he explains why he felt it necessary to step into another man's identity. And I have to admit I'm vaguely curious about how he managed to rig his questionnaire for Personal Connections."

Tyler frowned. "You're guessing. We don't know that he did that."

"Give me a break. No real guy would list *Gone with the Wind* as his favorite movie." He rolled his eyes. "And *Annie* as his favorite musical?"

Tyler felt the heat flood her cheeks. She'd already clenched her fists when the taxi suddenly lurched and she pitched forward against Nick's chest. His arms went automatically around her, and for a moment neither one of them moved. Tyler wasn't sure that she could. Their faces were very close, his mouth inches away. She had time to recall every single sensation of their kiss as she watched his lips slowly curve into a smile.

"I think you were about to deck me again, sugar," he said.

He was absolutely right, but the anger that had filled her had suddenly streamed away like sidewalk art in a rainstorm. In its place was that primitive response that only he could draw out of her. He touched and she wanted. It was as elemental and as frightening as that. She wanted him to kiss her again. She...*needed* that flash of heat, that quick, sharp spiral of desire. Curling her fingers into his shirt, she pulled him closer—

The cell phone rang...and rang again.

Nick swore as he set her firmly away and pulled the phone out of his pocket. "If it's your bridegroom, tell him that you'll only meet with him in a public place. Tell him the Palm Court at the Plaza."

She nodded as she gripped the phone. Somehow, she managed to flip it open. The minute she recognized the voice, she handed it to Nick. "It's Sam."

Turning, Tyler gazed out the window and tried to recapture her composure. As the cab stopped for a light, she recognized where they were. Rockefeller Plaza. The heat was having little effect on the number of tourists hurrying by. For one second, she felt an almost overpowering urge to open the door and run until she lost herself among them.

But Sheridans never ran away from their problems. It was racing down all those streets with Nick that must have put the thought in her mind. In spite of the heat, it had been fun. *Fun?* The traitorous little thought surprised her. She couldn't really be thinking of running away. She'd always accepted her responsibilities as a Sheridan. From the time she was eleven and her father had died, she'd known what she wanted: to run Sheridan Trust one day. He wouldn't be there to do it, so it was up to her. And it was steady, secure. Her grandmother had promised her it would always be there. People could fail you. One after another everyone she'd loved had left her. First her father, then her mother when she'd married again and left her with her grandmother. And now her grandmother, too. But her family's company would never leave. Leaning her head back against the seat, Tyler drew in a deep breath and made herself focus on what Nick was saying.

"I want you to send one of your operatives out to Kentucky. Once he gets to the Lawrence's horse farm, tell him to show that picture of the phony Richard to everyone in sight. He can say he's tracking down an heir for an insurance company.... Yeah, maybe it's a long shot, but maybe not. Put the plane ticket and the rental car on my credit card. And call me the minute you hear."

As Nick tucked the phone back in his pocket, Tyler said, "Why are you sending someone out to Kentucky? Why would Richard go there if he isn't really Richard? Have you changed your mind about him?"

Nick shook his head. "I'm operating on the theory that if you want to slip into someone else's identity, you have to know that person very well. If I'm right, someone out there should be able to identify who your bridegroom really is. Sam's operative ran into a dead end at the college. All they know is that someone went through four years there under Richard's name."

Tyler's mind began to race. "And if we get a name, his real name, we'll be able to trace him, won't we?"

"That's what I'm counting on."

"And that should give us some idea of why he's doing all this."

"Oh, I've got a good idea of why. I'm betting it will boil down to greed. Contrary to popular opinion, it's usually money and not love that makes the world go round."

The cell phone rang again. Taking it out of his pocket, he handed it to Tyler. "If it's your bridegroom..."

Tyler nodded. "The Palm Court." Flipping it open, she said, "Hello? Howard? No, I can't put Richard on because he's not with me. He's meeting me at the Plaza later."

Nick studied her as she made excuses to Howard for her bridegroom's continued absence. She was lying so skillfully that it was hard to believe how she'd panicked when she'd told the first one that morning. Harder still to believe that he'd known her only that brief span of time. He placed his hand against the back of the front seat to brace himself, as the driver lurched into the right turn lane. Then Nick turned to look at Tyler again. He wouldn't have known her at all if he'd stuck with his first decision to lock her out of his office. That would have been the smart thing to do.

Because everything she'd said was true. They were both smart people. They came from different worlds. She had her future all mapped out; and for the first time in his life, he actually had a plan for his.

And then there was the fact that the Sheridans didn't mix with the Romanos. Of course, it had been her grandmother who had lived by that rule. He'd never understood why his uncle had agreed to spend a lifetime of being someone Isabelle Sheridan could only fit into her life on selected weekends, someone she wouldn't ever introduce to her family.

What would Tyler's reaction be if he told her about her grandmother's affair with his uncle? he wondered. Disbelief? Shock? Disillusionment? He'd never know because he wouldn't tell her.

He'd also promised himself that he would never make the same mistake his uncle had. But every time he looked at Tyler, he could feel some of his resolve melting away. Clenching his fists, he fought against the urge to lift a damp strand of hair that had fallen across her cheek and tuck it behind her ear. He knew how soft her skin would feel, how it would heat as soon as he touched it. She was so incredibly responsive to a touch, a kiss. It made a man imagine exactly how her eyes might mist over, how her breath might catch, and what kind of sound she might make when he entered her for the first time. And the second. She was the kind of woman a man could lose himself in.

Lose himself. The words had a vivid memory slipping into his mind. He recalled standing with his uncle on the rooftop of the hotel. Henry was laughing, saying, *"You'll understand one day why I fell for Belle. When you meet that special woman, the one that you completely lose yourself in."*

Nick watched Tyler close the cell phone. No woman was going to lure him into a trap like that. He needed to get some distance, clear his head. For the first time in his life he felt the need for a plan. And the sooner he found her bridegroom for her, the better.

"I'm not going to be able to stall Howard much longer. He's beginning to worry because he can't get hold of Richard."

"Then let me do what you hired me for," Nick said.

"You have a plan?" she asked.

"I'm going to drop you off at my cousin's hotel, and then—"

"You're not going to drop me off anywhere. I'm going with you."

"We had this discussion before. Tyler Sheridan can't afford to get caught breaking and entering or any of the other things I might have to do."

"I'm willing to take the risk," she said.

Nick shook his head. "I work better alone."

"I know things about Richard that you don't. I could help." She reached out to place a hand on his arm. "Please. I have to do this. I need to know about Richard—about this man, whoever he is. If I was taken in by him, if I could have made that kind of mistake, perhaps my grandmother was right. Maybe I'm not enough of a Sheridan to run the company."

Nick's eyes narrowed. "Did she say that to you?"

Tyler glanced quickly away. "Not in so many words. But she was always warning me that I was too much like my mother. That I had her temperament, her tendency to be impulsive, her passion. She insisted that I learn control, but obviously she didn't think I'd succeeded or she wouldn't have left me on probation for a year." She turned back to him. "Please understand. I can't just sit in a hotel room and wait for your call."

He thought he'd steeled himself against any argument she might make, but what he saw in her eyes caught him off guard. Tears. Just the merest sheen, and she blinked them quickly away. Odd that her ability to control them made her seem more fragile to him than if the tears had fallen.

"I *won't* stay in that hotel. I'll look for Richard on my own."

"I intended to lock you in," he said.

"I'll scream. I'll..." As the sentence trailed off, she frowned. "You used past tense."

"Aha! The money your grandmother spent on fancy schools wasn't wasted, I see. They taught you grammar."

"Among other things," she said. "You're going to let me come with you. No tricks?"

Nick placed a hand over his heart. "Me? Pull a trick?"

"We *are* going to work together to find Richard, right? Just say yes or no."

"Yes. Against my better judgment." Then he leaned forward and spoke to the driver. "Let us out on the next corner."

"Does this mean you have a plan?" Tyler asked as he handed a bill to the cabdriver and opened the door.

"Nag, nag, nag. Is that all you CEOs do?"

"We need one," Tyler insisted as she stepped out onto the curb.

"How about this for starters? We're going to stop at an ATM and get some cash. That checkbook of yours isn't going to do us much good. C'mon—" taking her hand, he pulled her with him "—step lively."

5

"MAKE YOURSELF AT HOME. I'm just going to take a quick shower," Nick said, ushering Tyler into his apartment.

As he disappeared through a door in the opposite wall, Tyler concentrated on simply breathing. Walking up six flights in nearly airless heat had winded her. And though she wouldn't have thought it possible, it seemed even warmer in the apartment. The room, barely twelve by fifteen, was minimally furnished with a couch and a coffee table. Bookshelves lined one wall, and a counter with stools blocked off a kitchen area at one end.

She found a towel there, dampened it and dabbed at her forehead and temples. What she wouldn't give for a shower, she thought as a drip of sweat crawled down her back. Through the thin walls, she could hear Nick turn the water on. She wet the towel again and placed it at the back of her neck as a second and a third drop of perspiration followed the first. Closing her eyes, she let herself imagine just for a moment what it would be like to stand naked in that shower with the cold water pouring over her, the stream hitting her bare skin like pellets of ice.

Absolute heaven, she thought as she leaned back against the counter and let her mind drift with the fantasy. Picturing things in her mind was a game she'd often played as a child, especially whenever the rules of being a Sheridan prevented her from doing something she wanted. For a while, as she listened to the water in the next room, she imagined it raining on her. Gradually, she realized that she wasn't alone in the shower. Nick was there, too. And he looked as beautiful as he had that morning when she'd caught him sleeping. A sculptor's dream, with that face that belonged on a coin, those broad shoulders and chest slick with water. Unable to resist, she reached out her hand to touch him. What could it hurt? she thought as she ran her hand down his chest to the narrow waist, the flat stomach, and...oh, good heavens! Quite suddenly, the water was very hot, rising in steamy vapors all around her.

Opening her eyes, Tyler struggled again to breathe. The heat inside her was much more intense than what was pressing in on her in the stuffy room, and her legs were suddenly so weak she had to lean heavily against the counter. Curling her hands into fists, she concentrated on the small pain her nails made digging into her palms, and gradually the vividness of the image faded from her mind. What in the world was happening to her? The man didn't even have to be in the same room with her. She couldn't seem to stop herself from imagining what it might be like to...to be naked with him in a shower!

Slipping out of her jacket, she barely kept herself from throwing it across the room. What was it about Nick Romano that he could make her so angry one minute, so needy the next? If she could just figure it out, she could handle it. She *would* handle it.

Drawing in another deep breath, she folded her jacket neatly and placed it on the counter. Then she walked to the window and twisted the switch on the air conditioner. The initial blast of hot air made her step

quickly out of range, but the wheeze and rumble of the
motor drowned out the sound of the shower in the next
room. Satisfied, Tyler turned around and let her eyes
scan the apartment again. Before he walked through
that door, she was going to develop a plan to deal with
him. That had been the key to her success in handling
Sheridan Trust's board of directors for the past six
months. She'd never walked into a meeting without a
carefully mapped out strategy. There had to be some
clue here that would help her deal with Nick.

Moving first to the bookshelves, she glanced at a row
of books—two paperback thrillers, a worn volume of
poetry, the complete works of William Shakespeare,
and a cookbook that looked to be well thumbed
through. Curious, she opened it and found an inscrip-
tion on the flyleaf.

Nick,
I hope that someday you find a woman you want
to cook for.

Love,
Uncle Henry

An uncle who loved him. She envied him that. Setting the book down, Tyler glanced quickly at a row of
videotapes, each sporting a title of a cooking show.
Then she turned her attention to the framed photo-
graphs that filled the rest of the shelf. There was one of
a pretty dark-haired woman and two young girls who
appeared to be in their teens. They were all laughing at
someone or something beyond the camera. Lifting the
picture, she studied it more closely. She could see
Nick's coloring in both the girls, and the woman had his

eyes, dark and filled with laughter. Were these the sisters Nick had mentioned in the taxi?

The next photo was one of four men in tuxedos. It took her a second to recognize Nick because they all had the same coloring, the same finely crafted features. Each of them projected that hint of the warrior she'd glimpsed more than once in Nick, and the effect wasn't diminished one whit by the formal clothes. He hadn't mentioned brothers, but they all had to be related somehow, she decided as she set the picture down. She picked up another: a shot of Nick in-line skating with the two girls from the first photo. She scanned the rest quickly. They all seemed to be snapshots of Nick with family.

She didn't question the emotion that filled her. She envied him the closeness she saw in the photos. Here was the fun that she'd always imagined other people had with their families. How many times had she prayed for a sister or a brother? Or for a mother who had time—

Turning quickly, Tyler paced back to the window. That was old news, water under the bridge. On the street below, two little boys began to shove each other until one fell on his backside. The other dove on top of him. As they rolled across the sidewalk, a woman rose from where she was seated on the stoop and hurried to separate them. Tyler sighed. It was a waste of time to wish for things that you couldn't have. How many times had her grandmother said those very words to her?

Taking a deep breath, she watched the woman and the boys disappear into the brownstone across the street. What she did have was Sheridan Trust. And to keep it, she had to find Richard and discover what was going on.

Straightening her shoulders, she walked to the couch. She'd better focus on coming up with a plan to handle Nick Romano. Clearly, she couldn't afford to kiss him again. Shoving her hair back, she sat down. The problem was, she couldn't always figure out what he would do next. Her strategies for board meetings usually worked because everyone was so predictable. Nick Romano wasn't. He could goad her to fury one minute and make her laugh the next.

Was that why she found him fascinating? Tyler frowned. Perhaps Step One of her plan should be to stop thinking about him altogether. Deliberately, she switched her gaze from the framed photos to the neat stacks of newspapers in front of her. Picking the top one up, she discovered it had been folded to the crossword puzzle page. Searching through the other, she found they all were.

Working out the puzzles in the daily paper had always been one of the things she'd done to relax and escape. But she couldn't quite imagine Nick Romano hunched over a word game, chewing on the eraser of his pencil, throwing it against the wall in frustration. She smiled as the image filled her mind. Studying the one she was holding more closely, she saw that only a few spaces hadn't been filled in. Curious as to what had stumped him, she sat down. *Forty-five across.* She ran her finger quickly down the column.

NICK SLIPPED INTO a lightweight linen jacket, then checked himself in the mirror. In the khaki slacks and T-shirt, he could pass for either a tourist or a working New Yorker taking advantage of dress-down Friday.

He would willingly have given up the jacket, but it would provide necessary camouflage for his guns.

Frowning thoughtfully, he slipped his wallet and keys into his pocket. Usually taking a shower helped him to think, to clear his head. But not this time.

The case of the missing bridegroom just didn't make any sense. If the fake Richard was trying to shake down his bride-to-be, why use all the subterfuge? And why try to kidnap her? Not one part of that puzzle had fallen into place yet.

And he wasn't one bit closer to figuring out what to do about Tyler Sheridan. Glancing up, he met the eyes of the man in the mirror. He couldn't recall ever letting a woman worry him before. He'd always believed that when life sent you on a detour, you took it. Enjoyed it. And then you figured out a way to get back on course.

That was why he hadn't minded postponing college when his father died. It had only been a matter of putting his goals on hold for a time. *A dream deferred* is what poet Langston Hughes called it. Now the deferment was up. His goal was finally within reach. It might be costly, dangerous even, to take a detour at this time. Especially with a woman who was so out of his reach.

Straightening his shoulders, he sighed, then turned and walked to the door. She was a client, and treating her like one was the smart thing to do.

The moment he stepped out of the bedroom, the debate he'd been having with himself slipped right out of his mind. She was sitting on his couch, her head bent, her lips pursed as she scribbled a word into one of his crossword puzzles.

She looked just right.

A flood of emotions overwhelmed him. Though he couldn't identify them, he knew that something had changed, just as a slight shifting of light could change an artist's perception of a scene. He knew just that quickly that he wanted her, not just in his bed, but in his life. The realization left him shaken.

What if he couldn't have her? No, he wasn't going to think about that, nor was he going to dwell on the pricking that had begun in his thumbs. He was going to concentrate on the present, on what he had to do next. Reaching behind him, he pulled the door shut with a snap.

Tyler set the crossword puzzle down and turned to face him. "We have to talk."

"Sure thing," he said as he crossed to the counter that blocked off the kitchen area. A quick glance at her face told him that the ice princess was back. "You go ahead while I finish getting ready."

Tyler cleared her throat. "We never finished our discussion in the taxi about how we're going to handle the attraction we seem to feel for one another."

"I was just thinking the same thing. I suppose you have a plan all mapped out?" he asked as he pressed a lever, then waited for a panel to slide open.

"As a matter of fact, I do..." Her voice trailed off as she rose and moved quickly to join him at the counter. "Good heavens, that's a secret panel, isn't it? I've never seen one before."

Nick found himself smiling as she ran her hand down the side of the cupboard. When she turned to face him, he saw that the frost in her eyes had been replaced by curiosity and excitement.

"Was it here when you moved in?" she asked.

Nick shook his head. "One of my cousins built it for me. I keep guns here in the apartment. Sometimes my sisters stay overnight, and I don't want any accidents."

Tyler glanced around the room. "Where do they sleep?"

Nick grinned. "They bring sleeping bags, and we order in Chinese food. When they were younger, it used to be their idea of an adventure."

"They don't come over anymore?"

"Sure, but not as often. Grace just went out on her first date last month—a prom. I'm going to miss them," he said as he twisted the dials on a safe.

"You don't really want to move away, do you?"

"I wish I didn't have to." When she said nothing, but merely waited for him to continue, he said, "I'll never get away from the detective business if I stay here in New York. I know too many people who'll come to me, desperate because they have a problem. Just like you did this morning."

"Can't you just say no?" Tyler asked.

"Not to all of them. When you've been a PI for as long as I have, you build up a network of people you've done favors for. And they've done favors for you in return. There's never a time when the slate is wiped completely clean. If I want to practice law, I have to make a break."

"It's probably the only thing you can do," Tyler said.

There was understanding in her voice, a hint of regret in her eyes. Tilting his head slightly, he studied her for a moment. "You look like you've had to make some tough decisions of your own."

Just before she glanced away, he saw the sadness fill her eyes.

"I had to make a decision to leave my mother and live with my grandmother when I was eleven. It was shortly after my father died."

Reaching out, Nick lifted her chin so that he could see her eyes. "Whose idea was that?"

"It was a family decision. My grandmother wanted to make sure that I was raised as a Sheridan so that I could run the company someday. And my mother was about to remarry. We hadn't been seeing all that much of each other. She was very involved with this man, and he wanted her to join him in California. She and my grandmother decided together that it would be better if I stayed in Boston. I agreed."

It was altogether too easy to picture Tyler Sheridan, the child of eleven, being caught in a tug-of-war between two adults. He could even imagine her agreeing to it when she was told it was her duty as a Sheridan. It made him angry. "I suppose it was the smart thing to do."

Her gaze shifted from his. "Yes."

"The smart thing isn't always the best thing," he said as he dropped his hand. Then he removed his gun from the safe and checked the chamber.

"That's a gun," Tyler said.

"It's a nine-millimeter," he explained as he loaded it and slipped it into the holster he wore on his belt.

"I hardly think you'll be needing a weapon to look for Richard."

"That's another thing we have to talk about, sugar. I agreed to let you come along. But when it comes to the case, I'm the boss. What I say goes. Understand?"

She looked at him for a minute, then said, "With one exception. I'm not..." Her words trailed off when he took a second, smaller gun out of the safe. "Why do you need two guns? I hope you don't expect me to carry that."

Nick grinned at her as he slipped it into a specially

designed pocket in his jacket. "Nope. It's my backup gun, just in case someone relieves me of my other one." He tapped his pocket. "Just remember, it's right here if you want to borrow it."

"I don't believe in guns."

"And I don't believe in taking clients along on a case if they can't follow orders. So if you're the least bit uncomfortable about that, you can stay behind," he said as he removed a camera from the safe, then closed the panel.

Tyler's chin lifted, her eyes darkened. "I'll follow orders with one exception. I'm referring to the matter between us that we haven't settled yet."

"The fact that we want to make love?" Nick simply could not resist saying it.

"Things are *not* going to go that far between us," she said, rising to her feet.

"Really?" He stood up, too. The frost in her eyes was the next best thing to a dare and almost enough to make him throw caution to the wind. He satisfied himself by taking one step closer to her. She didn't move, didn't even flinch. "Maybe if I left for California right this moment, and maybe if we never saw one another again, we wouldn't make love. As it is, we're going to have to be very careful."

"In that particular area, I'll call the shots," Tyler said.

This time his grin erupted into a chuckle. "Absolutely. You've got yourself a deal, sugar. That's one area where I love it when a woman takes control. C'mon." Throwing an arm around her shoulder, he drew her with him out of the apartment.

TYLER STARED out the window of the taxi. Seated beside her, Nick had leaned his head back against the seat and closed his eyes. He was in his "mulling mode," he'd explained when she asked. Turning her head, she took a quick peek. His breathing was perfectly relaxed and even. And his face... Narrowing her eyes, she studied him more closely. "Mulling mode," indeed! Catching a quick nap was what Nick Romano was really doing. A piece of his hair had fallen across his forehead, and she had to fight the impulse to reach out and brush it off. Turning quickly away, she concentrated on the pedestrians hurrying around in the heat.

She envied him the nap. Her own mind was whirling with thoughts and images. The picture of her standing alone at the altar on the cover of the *Boston Globe* had become a permanent presence, popping up with annoying regularity.

Raising her hand, she rubbed against the headache that had taken root right behind her ear. She had just leaned back against the seat when a sudden lurch of the cab sent Nick sliding into her. Before she could prevent it, his head was on her shoulder.

She tried edging him back to his side of the seat, but it was like trying to move solid rock. So he *was* asleep. A quick elbow jab into his ribs would wake him, but she couldn't bring herself to do it. He looked peaceful, and with each breath he drew in and let out, some of that peace seemed to be stealing into her. Already, she felt a little less panic about the future. When they found Richard, she would figure out a way to handle the board. She had to. Outside the taxi, pedestrians raced about to get somewhere. She tried to swallow a yawn and failed. When her eyes drifted shut, she let her mind go blank, concentrating only on the coolness of the air-conditioning and the rock-solid strength of the man at her side.

"WAKE UP, SUGAR," said a low voice in her ear.

Tyler's eyes snapped open. "I wasn't asleep."

"Do you snore when you're awake?" Nick asked with a grin as he passed the taxi driver some money and opened the door.

She waited until they were on the sidewalk so that she could face him squarely. "You were the one who fell asleep. And don't you dare say you were just mulling things over."

"Are you always this cranky when you wake up?" he asked curiously.

"I..." she began, and then with a shake of her head, gave it up. "Did you by any chance come up with a plan?"

"Does this constant nagging work with your board of trustees?" he asked as he drew her with him through the lobby and into one of the elevators.

Tyler sighed and barely kept her foot from tapping as they shot upward to the floor that housed Richard's accounting firm.

"Okay, here's the plan," Nick said. "You're going to distract his secretary while I search Richard's office."

Tyler turned to him. "That's not a plan."

"Sure it is."

"Wait." She grabbed his arm as the elevator doors slid open. "At least tell me what I'm supposed to do to distract her."

"Improvise," Nick said, thrusting the camera he held into her hands. Then he led the way into a plushly carpeted reception area. Paneled wood lined the wall in front of them where a slim brunette of no more than twenty sat behind a desk. "Follow my lead. I'll get us past the first line of defense."

A smile bloomed on the young girl's face even as Nick approached. "Good afternoon, may I help you?"

"I'm Nick Romano from *Business Weekly*, and this is my assistant, Shirley." Removing a card from his pocket, he let the receptionist glance at it. "I have an appointment to meet with Richard Lawrence at three o'clock."

The young woman appeared to be seriously disappointed when she looked up at him. "I'm sorry, but Mr. Lawrence isn't in today."

Nick smiled. "He told me he would be out of the office most of the day, but that he'd make a special trip in to see me. Shirley's going to take some shots of the office. My editors want to run pictures with the article." Turning to Tyler, he said, "Why don't you start with one of Miss—" He turned questioningly to the brunette.

"Lieberman. Jenny Lieberman." She fluffed out her hair.

Tyler focused her camera and took three shots, while Nick asked Jenny Lieberman a few questions, teasing and laughing with her as he jotted down her answers in a small notebook he'd whipped out of a pocket.

"So I go straight down this corridor and then take a right?" Nick asked as he tucked his notebook away.

The brunette nodded. "How long do you think the interview will take? I'm finished at five."

"Sorry. Shirley and I have a deadline. How about a rain check for the beginning of the week? I just call the main number, right?"

"Sure," Jenny said, giggling when Nick winked at her.

"Isn't she a little young for you?" Tyler asked in a low voice, doubling her pace to keep up with him as they headed down the narrow hallway.

"Do I detect a note of jealousy, Shirley?"

"It was just an observation," Tyler said.

"Well, if you were observing that closely, you should have picked up enough to handle Ms. Armani. I'll take the camera, now."

Handing it to him, Tyler stared through the glass door at the person stationed at the desk in front of Richard's office. The large, middle-aged woman with square shoulders and iron-gray hair twisted into a bun was the perfect match to the voice Tyler had spoken to on the phone over the past four months.

"She's all yours," Nick whispered.

"Great," Tyler muttered. "You get to distract the teenybopper, and I get General Patton."

"If you're not up to it..." Nick began.

"Give me the business card," Tyler said. The moment he handed it over, she glanced down at it: N. Romano. Then she straightened her shoulders and opened the door. Ms. Armani continued writing in an appointment calendar even after Tyler had stopped in front of her desk. Out of the corner of her eye, Tyler saw that Nick had moved to a table near the entrance to Richard's office. Tyler summoned up a smile and held out her card. "Ms. Armani, I'm from *Business*—"

"I know where you're from," the woman said. "Ms. Lieberman told me she'd sent you down." Glancing up, she examined the card. "N. Romano. And the *N* stands for?"

"Nora," Tyler said.

Ms. Armani met her eyes for the first time, and Tyler felt as if they could see right through her. "You don't look Italian."

"My mother was pure Irish. I have an appointment to meet Mr. Lawrence at three."

"Not on his calendar, you don't." To prove her point, Ms. Armani turned around the calendar she'd been scribbling in.

"Perhaps he forgot to mention it to you," Tyler said, turning up the wattage on her smile.

The woman flicked a glance over her shoulder at Nick. He was flipping through a magazine. Then she turned her attention back to Tyler. "He never forgets to mention appointments to me. And there's no mention of *Business Weekly*, or N. Romano, or even a Nora on his calendar anywhere for the past month. I checked."

Over Ms. Armani's shoulder, Tyler saw Nick slip through the door of Richard's office just as the woman rose from her chair.

"I think you'd better leave now."

"I'm positive he said today at three," Tyler said quickly. "Surely it won't matter if I wait for a while. In the meantime, perhaps you could answer a few questions."

"I don't think so. It's against office policy for employees to give interviews unless they've been approved by one of the partners. And since you're not scheduled for any appointment, I'd have to check with them first." Reaching for the phone, she punched numbers in.

Tyler's mind began to race. Nick had only been in the office for a minute or so. He needed more time.

"Mr. Larrabie? This is Maude Armani in Mr. Lawrence's office. I have a Nora Romano here from *Business Weekly*. She claims she has an appointment for an interview.... No, there's no record of it on Mr. Lawrence's calendar. Yes, I'll bring them right down." She glanced at Tyler. "Mr. Larrabie will see you."

Tyler watched Ms. Armani hang up the receiver. *Stall*, she ordered herself. Once the woman noticed that

Nick was no longer in the room, the game was up. Her glance fell on the water carafe sitting on the edge of the desk. "Do you mind if I have a drink of water?" she asked.

"You can have one when we get to Mr. Larrabie's office," Ms. Armani said, rising from her chair.

Desperate, Tyler raised a hand to her head. "It's the heat. I've been walking around in it all day."

"If you and your associate will just—"

With the panic streaming through her, Tyler did the only thing she could think of. She sank bonelessly to the floor. For a moment, she thought she really had fainted. But the rapid pounding of her heart and the press of the carpet into her cheek convinced her she was conscious. Then she felt fingers pressing at her wrist, and a fresh spurt of panic shot through her. Would her pulse give her away?

"Oh, my," Ms. Armani said. "What should I...?" She removed her fingers from Tyler's wrist. "Oh, my."

Tyler felt the vibrations as the woman walked across the floor. She heard a door open. Then silence. Did she dare open her eyes? Holding her breath, she waited, counting the seconds as they ticked away. Another sound, closer this time, nearly had her jumping. Then she felt the press of fingers, this time at the pulse in her throat.

"Tyler, are you all right?"

It was Nick's voice, Nick's hands. Opening her eyes, she managed a grin. "I'm fine, but she'll be back any moment. I think she went to get one of the partners."

"What happened?" His hands gripped her shoulders, helping her to her feet.

"She didn't go for my story, so I pretended to faint. It

was the only thing I could think of to do. And it worked! It really worked!"

"Yeah." He urged her toward the door. "We'll celebrate once we get out of here."

"Did you find anything?" she asked, matching two steps to his one.

"I've got the cards from his Rolodex."

"Then your plan worked!"

"We'll see," Nick said as he winked and waved one last time at Jenny Lieberman and pulled Tyler onto the elevator.

NICK DIDN'T DARE SAY another word until the elevator had delivered them to the lobby and they'd made it out onto the street. For a moment there when he had stepped out of Richard's office and had seen Tyler lying on the floor, he was sure his heart had literally stopped. And his hand, when he'd reached to feel for her pulse, had been shaking. *Shaking!* Even now, he wasn't sure he had control of the feelings coursing through him. Because he wanted to shake *her.* Shoving his hands in his pockets, he struggled to gather his thoughts. Coolness had always been his trademark. And he knew better than most that emotional distance was the key to survival in his kind of business.

"I've never done that before—pretended to faint, I mean," she said, turning to him as they waited for a traffic light. Her face was flushed, her eyes bright with excitement.

"You enjoyed that, didn't you," he said.

"It was fun. I mean, I was scared at first when that old battle-ax was giving me the deep-freeze treatment, and I knew you hadn't had enough time in Richard's office. She was turning around, and I was sure she was going

to catch you. I think I stopped breathing. And then...I
just sank to the floor. When we were in college, Stevie
Hanover used to do that every time we had to dissect
something in Biology lab. But I never dared to try it before."

"Wait. Let me guess," Nick said dryly. "Sheridans
don't faint."

"No. But they're not supposed to lie, either. She
wanted to know what the *N* stood for on your card. I
told her Nora." Tyler snapped her fingers. "Just like
that."

Nick studied her for a moment. "You told her Nora,
did you? Why that particular name?"

Tyler shrugged as they started across the street. "It
just came to mind."

"You ever watch any of the old Thin Man movies on
late-night TV?"

"Sure—they're great...oh, you mean Nick and Nora
Charles? I love them. They made such a good team."

"Good team, my foot. She was always throwing a
monkey wrench into any case he was working on."

"Most of the time she was either *solving* the case he
was working on or saving his butt. Just as I saved yours
by fainting."

Nick shook his head. "For someone who claims she's
not supposed to lie, you're pretty good at telling whop-
pers!"

The ringing of the cell phone prevented Tyler from
replying, and at the sudden disappearance of the laughter from her eyes Nick almost swore. "Here," he said as
he flipped it open and handed it to her.

"Hello? He's right here," she said as she handed the
phone back to him.

"Yeah," Nick said, drawing her with him out of the

flow of pedestrians. Then he frowned as he listened to
what his friend Harry had to say. "Open it up." Turning to Tyler, he said, "A messenger service just delivered an envelope to your hotel. Harry's going to read it
to me." Suddenly, he frowned. "Say that again." After
listening carefully, he relayed the information to Tyler.
"It's a word-processed letter."

"What did it say?"

"'T.M.S., For the right sum you can have your bridegroom back in time for the wedding. Remember Scarlet
and Annie. R.J.L.'"

6

NICK RAISED HIS EYES from the letter that Harry had left for them at the desk to the woman seated next to him. Tyler hadn't stopped staring at it since they'd been seated at the table in the Palm Court. In the short taxi ride to the Plaza, she'd managed to lay on all of the control, the frosty distance, that she'd had when she'd first walked into his office that morning. Now she was a pale shadow of the animated, laughing woman who'd been talking to him on the street before her damn cell phone had rung. The only visible chink in her armor was that she'd been stirring her tea for two straight minutes.

Right now he would have given almost anything to bring the laughter back to her eyes. He reached for his coffee and drained it, then glanced around the room. It was Friday afternoon, time for high tea, and tables were nearly filled. Violin music could be heard above the soft buzz of conversation. At the table next to theirs, a woman was helping her young daughter select a tiny sandwich from a china plate. In his mind he could picture Isabelle bringing Tyler here when she was just that age. It was a perfect setting for them both. At the table beyond, a man and woman were holding hands and sipping champagne. The woman was wearing a suit not unlike Tyler's, and the guy could have stepped right off the pages of a men's fashion magazine.

This was Tyler Sheridan's world, all right. At least,

that's what he would have said six hours ago. He shifted his gaze back to the woman sitting next to him. But she'd surprised him. Inside that cool armor that she'd so carefully pulled into place was another woman. One who'd fake a faint on the spur of the moment. One who, with a little practice, would have a hell of a right cross. One who tasted like some exotic dessert that a man could never get enough of. It might be the biggest mistake of his life, but he wasn't about to let that woman slip away from him.

And right now, she was stirring that tea as if she wanted to lose herself in the whirlpool she was creating in her cup.

"Tyler," he said, reaching over to still her hand.

She carefully placed her spoon on her saucer and glanced up at him. "Everything's changed."

"What?"

"Richard's been kidnapped, and that changes everything."

"Whoa, slow down," Nick said. "We don't know for sure that he's been kidnapped."

Tyler tapped her finger on the letter Harry had given them when they'd arrived. "That's a ransom note. You said so yourself."

"What if Richard is the one sending it?"

As Tyler stared at him, a faint line appeared on her forehead. "You think he'd fake his kidnapping so that he could extort money from me?"

"Whoever sent it is using the same language that was used in the ad—and you were sure Richard placed that."

"But he couldn't—" She shook her head. "You don't know Richard."

"I know that he's a man who's spent the past ten

years masquerading as someone else. That makes him a liar and a thief."

She didn't flinch, she didn't argue with him, either. But her skin paled, and Nick felt as if he'd kicked another puppy. "Look, I'm sorry."

Tyler pressed a hand to her temple. "No, you're just doing your job. What did you find in his office?"

"I lifted some prints off his telephone. If he's got a record, Sam will be able to get a name. We can drop them off at his office just as soon as we look through the cards I took from his Rolodex. Are you up to doing that?"

Nodding, Tyler reached for her cup, took a sip and frowned. "It's cold."

"That'll happen when all you do is stir it for three minutes." He signaled a waiter. "I'll get you a fresh pot."

"No. I'll have whatever you're having."

His brows rose. "I thought you didn't do caffeine."

Tyler's chin lifted. "This is my day for trying new things."

Nick's grin widened as he turned to the waiter. "Two cappuccinos." As soon as the young man hurried off, he handed her half the stack of cards he'd taken out of the Rolodex.

"What am I looking for?"

"Anything that strikes you as odd or doesn't seem to fit."

A few minutes later, Tyler reached for the cappuccino that the waiter had just delivered. "I didn't see anything unusual in my pile."

Nick handed her a card as he switched the stacks. "This Howard Tremaine at Sheridan Trust— I assume he's the same Howard who keeps calling you?" At Tyler's nod, he continued, "Why would Richard have both his office and home phone numbers?"

"Howard was acting as a stand-in best man, making all the wedding arrangements in Boston, because Richard's friend Mark Donavon isn't going to get in from Louisville until next Friday."

"Louisville? He comes from the same place as the real Richard. You didn't mention that before."

"I didn't think of it. Is it important?"

Nick rubbed his thumbs and fingers together. "I have a feeling it might be. Have you ever met this guy Donavon or talked to him on the phone?"

This time when Tyler shook her head, Nick slipped her cell phone out of his pocket. "I'm going to call Sam and fill him in on everything. He can have the man he sent out to Kentucky try to locate this Mark Donavon. See if you can find a phone number in those cards."

Tyler began to make her way through the second pile of cards. With a part of her mind, she tried to concentrate on the conversation Nick was having with his cousin. But Nick's side of it consisted mostly of frowning and grunting, which didn't bode well. She turned over another card. *Look for something that doesn't fit.*

But *nothing* fit. Richard, the con man? Richard, the kidnap victim? Neither image fit the man she'd known for the past four months—the man she thought she'd fallen in love with. Then the thought struck her. If he'd really been kidnapped, it might not be such an easy matter to get him back.

Kidnappers seldom released their victims. Usually they killed them.

"Did you find a number for Donavon?" Nick asked.

"What?" She glanced up from the cards.

"Mark Donavon's phone number?"

She shook her head.

"Sam, we don't have a number. I'll talk to you soon." Slipping the cell phone into his pocket, he studied Tyler. "What's up? Did you find something?"

"No. I was just thinking that if Richard or whoever this man is has really been kidnapped, his life could be in danger. Can't we do more than just wait for Sam to come up with something?"

Nick frowned. "I wouldn't get too worried about your bridegroom yet."

"I know you think he's set this up just to get money. But someone else could be after the money, too. A lot of people might figure I would pay a lot not to be left—"

The pressure of Nick's hand on her arm stopped her from completing her thought. His voice was pitched low when he spoke. "Careful. These tables are set close together."

Tyler drew in a deep breath. "You're right. It's just that I've been worrying about myself. And it's Richard who might be—"

"I told you before. It's not time to worry about him yet. Not when Sam suspects he might have a good reason for staging this whole thing. He thinks your Richard has a gambling problem."

Tyler straightened in her chair. "He's wrong."

"Maybe. But it would explain why he's broke."

"That can't be true. Richard always insisted on paying for everything when we went out. He even picked up the bill when I stayed here at the Plaza. And the initial fee at Personal Connections was ten thousand dollars."

Nick shrugged. "He might have seen that as a good investment. The facts are he has no money in the bank, and his credit cards are maxed out at the fifty-thousand dollar level. It's harder to trace any loans he might have from less legitimate lenders."

Tyler shook her head. "Debt doesn't equal a gambling problem."

"It could if you regularly visit racetracks—and according to his credit card receipts, that's what this Richard guy has been doing."

For a moment, Tyler didn't speak. Finally she said, "If he's got a gambling problem and he's in debt, he must have had this in mind all along. Get engaged to a rich woman, then fake a—"

The rest of her sentence was cut off when he covered her mouth with his. She lifted a hand to his shoulder to shove him away. But it was too late. The heat of his mouth, the response that tore through her, wiped the intention right out of her mind, and she curled her fingers into his jacket to pull him closer. This was what she wanted, what she needed. Just as she moved toward him, ready to demand as well as give, his mouth abruptly softened on hers, his tongue gently soothing hers as he drew back.

"Sorry, sugar. You make a man forget where he is."

She stared at him. She had to concentrate just to breathe. If his hands hadn't been on her shoulders, supporting her, she wasn't sure she could have remained upright in her chair. What had she been saying? It wouldn't come back to her. All she could hear was the violin music. *Violins!* She was in the middle of the Palm Court in the Plaza Hotel, and nearly everyone was staring at her!

"I hope you're not thinking of decking me again," Nick said.

Tyler drew in a deep breath and managed to keep her

clenched hands in her lap. "People are staring at us," she managed through gritted teeth.

Nick leaned closer, pitching his voice low. "Because we kissed. They were already glancing our way before we did that. Would you rather they overheard what you were about to say?"

"The last time I caused a scene in the Palm Court, I was ten. I spilled my tea."

Taking one of her fists, Nick kissed the knuckles. "This was more fun, don't you think?"

She fought against the urge to smile at him. "You're..." With a sigh, she shook her head. "Never mind. What should we do next?"

"That's a loaded question, sugar, when you have a suite upstairs."

"That's not what I meant." And it wasn't. But for a moment, the image of what it might be like filled her mind. Even as it did, she saw the teasing light in his eyes replaced by something darker and more reckless.

"Tell me what you're thinking," he coaxed softly.

It was dangerous to keep looking into those eyes. They promised everything.

"Tell me," he repeated.

"I wish I could be someone else—someone who could..."

"...sneak upstairs and make love just for the fun of it," he finished.

Those eyes could read her innermost thoughts, even her fantasies. They could hypnotize her. And if he asked her right now...or even if he didn't ask her, but merely rose and drew her with him, she would follow.

Nick leaned closer. "When I do make love with you, it will mean a lot more than that. And you won't be pretending to be someone else. It will be just you and me."

The phone rang twice before either one of them moved. Nick picked it up from the table and handed it to her.

"Yes?" She was surprised at how normal her voice sounded when she spoke into the mouthpiece. She was even more surprised at the voice she heard. It was a woman's voice, soft and deep pitched. Tyler shot Nick a curious look as she passed the phone to him.

"Yeah?" He said nothing more for a moment or two, but the smile that had initially bloomed on his face gradually faded into a frown. "No, of course, I hadn't forgotten. It's just that... Yeah, I know I can't miss it. Well, Sam was wrong, and she isn't distracting me. And she's not a date. She's a client." The frown faded. "So she's a pretty client. That's not a crime." He threw back his head suddenly and laughed. "Yes, I'll ask her to come with me." The second he cut the connection, he turned to Tyler. "My mother wants you to come to this going-away party my family is throwing for me. Sam told her I might forget all about it."

"A going-away party? I don't want to intrude."

"Nonsense," Nick said as he scooped the Rolodex cards back into his pocket. "I'm not leaving you alone."

She made one last effort as he dropped bills on the table and rose. "I don't have anything to wear. This suit..." She found herself talking to his back as he pulled her along through the lobby of the Plaza.

"Not to worry. My mother runs a dress shop."

TYLER WASN'T SURE which surprised her most, the exclusive little dress shop that opened off the lobby of Henry's Place, a small hotel on the Upper East Side, or Nick's mother. The hotel belonged to his Uncle Henry's sons, the three cousins she'd seen in the photos—Sam,

A.J. and Tony. Nick had filled her in on that much during the short taxi ride. But when he'd introduced her to Gina Romano, Tyler had immediately recognized her as the slim brunette in the photos whom she'd assumed was Nick's older sister. Saying so had earned her a warm hug from Gina and a chuckle from Nick. And then Gina had shooed Nick out of her shop, reminding him that he had to hold up the family honor in the basketball game that was about to start on the roof.

"Basketball?" Tyler asked when she and Gina were alone.

"It's a disease in this family. Do you play?"

"Not since college."

"Well, you're probably safe from being recruited this evening. Since this will be Nick's last game for a while, the Romano men have been challenged by the Costellos to a championship match. That's probably all we'll have time for before dinner. But on holidays, we all have to play." She smiled and shrugged. "I think it's in the blood. Now—" narrowing her eyes, she studied Tyler from head to toe "—Nick tells me you need some play clothes, that all you have to wear are those suits."

Tyler felt the heat rise to her cheeks. "I work a great deal of the time."

Moving forward, Gina took her hands and squeezed them. "I'm sorry. I didn't mean that as a judgment or criticism. It's good to work a lot. But tonight you'll be more comfortable, I think, in something less businesslike." Drawing Tyler with her, she led the way through a curtain at the back of her shop. The narrow room was filled with racks of dresses. Gina quickly selected several. "Let's try these. If you don't like them, there are a lot more."

Minutes later, Tyler found herself in a tiny dressing

room, staring at someone she hardly recognized in the mirror. In the red slip dress with the embroidered hem, she didn't look anything like the Tyler Sheridan who ran board meetings.

"What do you think?" Gina asked, as Tyler stepped out. "Turn around."

Tyler did as she was told. Gina had insisted she try on a pair of matching sandals, and she felt a little like Cinderella must have felt before the ball. "I've never seen anything like this dress. This stitching looks as if it was done by hand."

"It was. I do some of the work myself. The rest I job out to women from my old neighborhood."

"You're a designer?" Tyler turned to study Nick's mother.

Gina beamed at her. "It's been my dream to have someone call me that. Everything in the shop is one of a kind."

"Have you thought of expanding?"

"It's the next step of my dream. When my husband first died, my brother-in-law Henry invited me to move in here and run a gift shop in his lobby. First I had to make sure the shop turned a profit. After a while, I started saving, and with Nick's help—" she waved a hand "—I've gotten this far."

"It must have been hard," Tyler said.

"I couldn't have done it without family."

Tyler glanced thoughtfully at the piles of clothes they'd decided against, and she thought of how they might appeal to younger women. "You know, I think I might be able to help you expand."

From the main room of the shop came the sound of a bell ringing.

"Mom, where are you?" a breathless voice asked.

"Nick said..." another young voice said. "We came to see—ouch! Don't pinch!"

"Speaking of family, I think I hear my daughters," Gina explained as she slipped out through the curtains to the front.

"Mom, where is she? And tell Grace to stop pinching!"

"Grace, stop pinching," Gina said automatically, as Tyler joined them. The moment she did, the two young women stopped talking to merely stare at her. They both had their brother's eyes, intelligent, penetrating. The younger one—Tyler guessed her to be about fourteen—had his unruly curls. The taller one had her mother's straight hair, and it fell in a sleek line to her shoulders. Each had a full share of the Romano family good looks.

"You'll have to pardon my daughters," Gina was saying. "Nick has never brought one of his dates home before."

"Oh, but I'm not his date. I'm a client," Tyler said, moving forward to take the hand the older girl was holding out to her.

"I'm Grace," she said. "And this is Lucy."

"Tyler."

"Tyler." Lucy seemed to be tasting the name on her tongue. "I *love* that name. Lucy is so...plain."

Grace rolled her eyes. "She complains about her name every day. I told her she can get it legally changed."

Lucy whirled on her sister. "Maybe I'll just do that."

"Girls." Although Gina's voice was soft, Grace and Lucy immediately quieted. "It's rude to argue in front of Miss..." Glancing at Tyler, she said, "Nick didn't mention your last name."

"Sheridan," Tyler supplied. "But I'd much rather be called Tyler."

"Sheridan?" Gina looked at her for a moment before she turned back to Lucy and Grace. "Go on back up to the roof. Someone has to play hostess and welcome the guests until I can change and get up there. Okay?"

The moment the girls had left the shop, Tyler turned to Gina. "Could you tell me why you looked at me the way you did when I mentioned my last name?"

"I didn't mean to look at you in any particular way," Gina said.

"But you did," Tyler insisted. "It's the same look that Nick gets in his eyes whenever he mentions my grandmother."

"Then you are Isabelle Sheridan's granddaughter? I can't see a resemblance."

"But that's not what you were thinking a moment ago. I know not everybody liked her."

Reaching for her hand, Gina gave it a squeeze. "I'm sorry for your loss. I know how hard it is to lose someone you love."

"Please, tell me what it is that she did to make Nick look... I don't even know how to put it into words. But when I first walked into his office, he didn't want to take the case. And it wasn't just because he was packing. I had to bully him."

Gina's brows rose. "You bullied Nick? I wish I'd been there. As far as his feelings for your grandmother go, all I can say is he was very close to his Uncle Henry."

"What was my grandmother's connection to Henry Romano?"

Gina frowned. "I've said too much. Nick is the one you should be asking. If you do, I'm sure he'll tell you."

WATCHING A BASKETBALL GAME on the roof of a hotel was the last thing she'd expected to be doing when she'd flown into Manhattan the day before. But then the rooftop was really more like a park. A penthouse apartment took up one corner, and a garden filled another. Tony, one of Nick's cousins, was the chef at the hotel, and he grew his own vegetables, along with prize-winning roses that filled pots and wound their way up trellises. Five picnic tables had been lined up in a row to form bleachers along a tarmac-covered court. The spectators, over a hundred by her quick calculation, alternated between cheering and shouting their complaints to the players.

"Would you like some more wine?" Grace asked, taking advantage of a momentary lull.

"No, thanks." Tyler turned to smile at the young girl. Lucy sat on her other side. They'd taken charge of her from the moment she'd stepped onto the roof, introducing her to relatives and friends of Nick. The way everyone hugged her and welcomed her, she felt that she ought to correct their misconception that she was Nick's date. But before she could even try, the girls would whisk her off to the next group of guests.

A sudden shout went up from the crowd, and Tyler glanced up just in time to see the ball leave Nick's hands, rise in a graceful arc and then plummet through the hoop.

"A net ball!" Lucy screamed, tugging on her arm. "Did you see it? It didn't even touch the rim! Nick can do those all the time."

Yes, she had seen it. Because, except for that moment when she'd turned to answer Grace's questions, she'd barely taken her eyes off Nick Romano since the game had started. There was something about all the Romano men. Shirtless, wearing shorts or cutoffs, they all reminded her of Greek and Roman sculptures she'd seen in museums. Except these men were real. Tony was the tallest and leanest; A.J., the cop, was the quickest; and Sam, the youngest of the four men, was the sneakiest. But Nick was by far the best player. And the opposing team seemed to agree with her, since they were double-teaming him.

"Nick's very good," Grace said as soon as there was another lull in the noise.

Lucy tugged on her other arm. "Do you like him?"

"Lucy, you're not supposed to ask—"

"It's all right," Tyler said. "I like him very much."

"Do you think you could talk him into staying here in New York? I don't want him to go to California," Lucy said.

Tyler laid a hand on the young girl's arm. "Your brother and I...we're not seeing each other. I'm just a client."

"Oh," Lucy said, the disappointment clear in her voice.

"She shouldn't have asked you that," Grace said. "Mom says we can't talk about it, and we can't ask him to stay. He's done so much for us, and this job means everything to him. You know that Lucy."

Tyler turned back to the younger girl. "You're not going to lose him, you know. He'll visit, and he'll invite you out to California. He loves you very much."

To her surprise, Lucy's hand somehow found its way into hers.

Suddenly, Grace jumped to her feet and shouted, "Foul! That's a personal foul!"

Tyler rose too, and for a moment she was sure her heart had stopped beating. Nick was lying full length on the court, and he wasn't moving. Around her the crowd had joined Grace's chant of "foul," but Tyler couldn't speak. Finally, the referee turned and made a signal with his hands. Nick still didn't stir.

She wanted to run down to him. But she wasn't sure she could budge. And neither Grace nor Lucy seemed concerned.

Grace was jumping up and down, cheering the ref's decision. "A personal foul! That means he gets two free throws! Way to go, Nick!"

Couldn't anyone see that he was still lying on the court? "He's hurt," she finally managed. "Somebody should do something."

"Gerry Costello elbowed Nick in the stomach. He does that all the time, the sneak!" Grace explained. "But Nick's got an iron stomach. He used to let Lucy and me walk on it when we were little. He can take anything! You watch, he'll be up in a minute."

Grace wasn't even finished talking when Nick rolled to his feet, and the crowd began to cheer. Tyler pressed a hand to her heart to make sure it had started beating again. This was just a basketball game. She was being ridiculous. As Nick walked easily to the free throw line, her eyes narrowed. Grace was right. He didn't seem injured at all. He'd probably been faking it. As she studied him, he bounced the ball twice, and then he turned. The grin he shot her was cocky, arrogant, and as his eyes met hers, she was absolutely sure her heart did stop. Then the ball left his hands and swished through the net.

She surged to her feet with the rest of the spectators and screamed. "A net ball!" She turned to Lucy. "Did you see it? A net ball!"

IT WAS HOURS before Tyler found herself a moment alone to think. The party had begun to wind down, and her head was spinning with a kaleidoscope of events and impressions. From a fairly quiet corner of the rooftop, she gazed out over Manhattan. Night had finally fallen, but the city with its millions of lights waged a valiant fight against the darkness. Even the rooftop of Henry's Place was doing its part. The picnic tables were aglow with candles, and the basketball court had long since been converted into a dance floor lit with Chinese lanterns. For the past hour, the guests had reluctantly begun to depart. Gina was seeing an elderly couple on their way, and Nick was dancing with Lucy. A Strauss waltz poured out of the speakers as he whirled her around the tarmac.

His sisters might not have been able to talk to him about their feelings, but Nick knew what they were going through. He'd danced with them frequently during the evening. Grace and he had done a tango earlier that had made all the other dancers fade to the sidelines so they could watch. He'd even jitterbugged with Gina. He was a man of many talents. The only person he hadn't danced with was Tyler.

Not that she was jealous. She was his client, not his date as everyone seemed to assume. Although he hadn't done much to correct that impression at dinner when he'd insisted she sit next to him at the head of the picnic table. The meal had been nothing like the formal events she was used to at her grandmother's house. Instead, platter after platter had been passed around— veal, chicken, beef, shrimp and more pasta dishes than she could remember the names of. Nick had insisted that she try each one because it was a specialty that one of the guests had brought to share.

"It would be impolite to refuse," Nick had whispered in her ear.

Now she pressed her hand against her stomach. She'd eaten more than she ever had in her life. And it had been delicious. But she still wasn't sure which she'd enjoyed more—the food or the round robin of stories that the Romanos and their friends had offered up as entertainment. Each storyteller had exaggerated or elaborated, she was sure, some humorous incident from Nick's past.

She'd learned a lot about him over the course of the evening. She'd already known that he was brave and kind. But it seemed he was generous, too. Though he'd obviously earned a good living in the PI business, he also did *pro bono* work, once tracking down a stray dog for the sum total of a dollar and thirty-two cents. Her lips curved as she recalled the story. It was all the client had been able to tip out of his piggy bank, and Nick had accepted it as payment in full.

He was now leading Lucy off the dance floor to where his mother was standing at the exit to the stairs. He would dance with Gina next, and then it would be Grace's turn again.

He was a very complex man. It occurred to Tyler then that she'd learned more about him in the course of a day than she'd learned about Richard in four months. In spite of the Personal Connections questionnaire and months of dating, she hadn't known the man who was pretending to be Richard James Lawrence at all.

And now he might be kidnapped.

She glanced down at her finger where she'd worn his ring. Any impression of its existence had faded long ago. There was a good chance that the future she'd worked so hard for would disappear just as easily, and she hadn't come up with a plan. She hadn't even thought of her bridegroom or Sheridan Trust in hours.

"Let me guess. You're making a plan."

She turned to find Nick standing next to her. "I feel as if I should be doing something."

"You're worrying." Raising his hand, he drew one finger down the space between her brows. "Did you know there's a little line that forms here every time you do?"

"I want to do something besides worry."

Nick grinned. "I have a suggestion."

She tried to ignore the smile tugging at the corners of her mouth. "I was talking about coming up with a plan."

"How can we possibly come up with a plan before we know what the kidnappers or your bridegroom want? On the other hand, I do have a suggestion for making the time fly while we're waiting for them to contact us."

One possibility raced through her mind, jolting her system. "I don't think so."

"Relax," he said taking her hand. "I think I want to settle this bridegroom problem once and for all before I make love to you. In the meantime, let's dance."

7

"I'M NOT MUCH of a dancer," Tyler said.

"You were doing all right with A.J. and Tony and Sam." He'd pulled each one of his cousins over for a little talk afterwards. Drawing her with him, he ducked behind a trellis and pressed the button on the penthouse elevator.

"Where are we? The dance floor's back there."

"I have a place I want to take you to."

"Now? We can't. What if the kidnappers try to get in touch with us? It's—" she paused to glance at her watch "—eleven forty-five. That's nearly tomorrow."

He tapped the cell phone in his pocket. "If they send a message to the Plaza, Harry will call us. And I doubt they'll be calling at the stroke of midnight. They want you tense and worried so you'll do what they say."

"Your family—"

"My mother was the one who suggested that we sneak out the back way. Lucy nearly dozed off twice in my arms during that last dance. She doesn't want the evening to end."

"She doesn't want her brother to leave," Tyler said.

The understanding in her eyes had the need building in him to touch her, to really touch her. He satisfied himself by running a finger down the earring she was wearing. "We both need to escape—just for a little while. So here's the plan."

Her brows rose. *"You've* got a plan?"

"I can be a very methodical kind of guy," he said as the elevator doors slid open and he urged her through them.

Her unladylike response made him grin. "I'd be willing to bet that Sheridans don't snort."

"I've done a lot of things Sheridans don't do since I met you."

Nick raised her fingers to his lips. "It's just the beginning, sugar."

Her hand was trembling as she drew it away and lowered it to her side. "Let's hear the plan."

"We get in a taxi and go to this dance club I know."

Tyler was shaking her head as the elevator stopped and the doors opened. "And? What happens when we get to the club?"

Nick shot her a grin. "We enjoy living in the moment."

THE CELL PHONE RANG just as they got out of the cab. Music was pouring through the open door of the club, so Nick steered Tyler into the shelter of the nearest doorway. She didn't immediately reach for the phone. "Do you think it could be the kidnappers?"

"I don't think so."

The phone rang for the second time.

"If it is," Nick continued, "try to keep them talking. Concentrate on the voice and see if you can recognize it. Make the caller repeat everything. Got it?"

She nodded, taking the phone as it rang for the third time. "Hello?"

Nick saw the immediate easing of the tension in her shoulders.

"Howard? I can hardly hear you..." A burst of static

exploded in her ear that even he heard. "What?" To Nick she said, "He's in Manhattan, but I can hardly hear him— What? 422...422-5718." Lowering the phone, she punched in numbers. "I'm going to call him back and see if we can get a better connection. Howard? It's a little better. What are you doing in New York? No, I'm not at the Plaza. I'm out dancing. And Richard's in the men's room right now."

Leaning against a plate-glass window, Nick studied her. Just that morning in the park she'd stumbled over the story she was making up. Now the lies were rolling off her tongue. Then suddenly, he saw the tension return to her shoulders.

"Of course, the wedding is going to go off on schedule. There's absolutely nothing to worry about. Good night, Howard."

Taking the phone, Nick slipped it back into his pocket, counting to ten as he did so. When he trusted himself to speak, he said, "You're not going to marry that guy even if he does manage to come out of this smelling somewhat like a rose."

She met his eyes squarely. "No."

One word, just one simple word, and the anger that had been building in him flowed out like water. "You'll have to tell Howard that sooner or later."

Her chin lifted. "I'll tell him when I inform the rest of the board. He's been running interference for me with them ever since my grandmother died. I've come to rely on his advice, his support. But this is one thing I have to handle for myself."

"You sound like your grandmother."

Immediately, she frowned. "I'm not sure you mean that as a compliment. You didn't like her very much, did you."

"Did anyone really like Isabelle Sheridan?" he asked as he took her hand and drew her back on the sidewalk.

She stopped and turned to face him. "That's not an answer. It's just another question. I asked Gina what it is you have against my grandmother, and she said to ask you."

They'd gotten close enough to the open door of the club for the music to surround them, for the flickering light to play over her skin. She looked fragile, vulnerable. "I'll tell you later. Right now, let's stick to my plan. For the next hour, we live totally in the now. We pretend that Isabelle Sheridan and your ex-bridegroom don't exist."

After a second's hesitation Tyler nodded, and he drew her with him through the doorway. Almost immediately, they were swallowed up by the crowd. Nick ran interference, cutting a path through wave after wave of people until he reached the stairwell to the lower level. Holding tightly to her hand, he started down. A bar ran the length of one of the walls. In front of it, people stood three deep, hip to hip. The band gyrated on a raised platform at the far end of the room, but the music roared from speakers in each corner. Directly in front of them, a small dance floor formed a tiny island in a sea of tables. Nick wedged himself through a tangle of arms and legs, until he reached the center. Then at last, he pulled Tyler into his arms.

For a moment he merely held her close and absorbed the sensation. He'd been wanting to touch her since the moment she'd walked out on the roof. He'd imagined how her skin would heat beneath the thin silk of the dress. He ran his hands over her hips, urging her closer.

"Nick..."

Lowering his head, he pressed his cheek against hers. "You'll have to speak up."

"This isn't dancing."

She had a point. It was more like some exquisite kind of torture. Drawing her even closer, he moved against her. "It's one kind of dancing." Then, unable to resist, he tasted the skin at her shoulder. The flavor, warm and sweet, did nothing to satisfy his hunger. It only increased it. Scraping his teeth along her collarbone, he absorbed the shudder that moved through her, and wanted more.

"Nick...we can't do this." She wasn't moving away. Her mouth was still at his ear, and her hands had moved around his neck, her fingers into his hair.

"But we are," he said as he closed his teeth on her earlobe.

"We're in public."

"Mmm."

His breath in her ear was doing things to her equilibrium. Tyler held onto him more tightly and tried to focus. "There are...people here."

"Who aren't paying one bit of attention."

He was right. In the part of her mind that hadn't completely turned to mush, Tyler could see that no one was. Each couple on the dance floor was either lost in the music or in each other. The sound poured over them, through them, in some kind of erotic, jungle rhythm that mimicked the pumping of her blood. She had to move away...while she still could. Then his lower body moved against hers, and she felt the arrow of heat shoot through her, destroying the last remnant of her resolve. If he hadn't been holding her so tightly, she was sure she would have melted into a puddle at his feet. Or perhaps just evaporated into steam and blown away.

"We—we're going to be arrested," she finally managed.

"They'll have to get to us first. Kiss me."

She hesitated, caught between desire and prudence. Heaven and hell. The music slowed abruptly to a softer, more seductive rhythm.

"It won't go any farther. Not in this crowd," Nick said.

It wasn't his words that convinced her. It was the betrayal of her own body. Suddenly, kissing Nick was what she wanted, all she wanted. Her head seemed to turn of its own volition, and she pressed her lips to his. He drew back once, then again, teasing her before he covered her mouth with his. One last coherent thought streamed through her mind. *It felt like coming home.* Then her mind emptied completely and all she could do was feel. There was so much softness in his mouth, so much heat—she wanted nothing more than to lose herself in it. But there were so many flavors, tempting her to sample them. And she did, with her tongue and her teeth. It was sweetness she tasted first. It reminded her of a melting ice cream cone, one she had to keep licking and licking so that not one drop could escape. And beneath that was a deeper flavor. *Hunger.* Was it his or hers? She didn't know, didn't care. She simply wanted more. Exploring it, she savored the deepening richness as hunger changed slowly into demand. The beat of the music quickened then—or was it just that it seemed to be inside her, flowing through her—?

As abruptly as his mouth had hardened on hers, it softened and withdrew.

"No. Don't stop."

"Shh," he whispered in her ear, then moved his

mouth to rain gentle kisses over her face. "I think we need to take a little break."

Little by little, reality crept into the fog of sensations that had enveloped her. One thing seemed very clear. If they hadn't been on a crowded dance floor, she wouldn't have let him stop. That one realization was enough to stiffen her spine. What in the world was happening to her? She drew back until she could see his face. "I've never done anything like this before."

"Must be you're a natural."

"I think we should leave."

He leaned close so that she could hear every word. "Do you know what we'd be doing if we weren't here?"

She stiffened again. She *knew.* Already, she was beginning to picture it in her mind, feel it—

Then suddenly he swung her out and pulled her back into his arms. "Let's dance."

Tyler blinked. "I don't know how."

Nick grinned at her. "Tyler Sheridan doesn't know how? Pretend you're Nora again. Would she let the Thin Man outdo her?"

No, Nora wouldn't. And neither would she, Tyler decided. How hard could it be? Moving a little back from him, she tried to imitate what he was doing. But it was harder than it looked, and it didn't help that other dancers were bumping against her. Frowning, she concentrated harder, moving her hips one way and then the other. But she had to move her arms at the same time. That seemed to be essential. When she raised her hand, Nick drew her close enough to say, "Relax. Try to feel the beat."

The beat was hard to miss, since the floor and even

the air seemed to be vibrating with it. Once again, she started to move the lower part of her body. That was where Nick seemed to be incredibly flexible. He was very good. And he was right. Relaxation was definitely the key. And the less she tried to plan out each separate movement, the smoother each seemed to become. Closing her eyes for a moment, she tried to let the beat of the music take over until it was one with her legs, her arms, her body.

The memory slipped into her mind of a morning she'd been dancing for her father, whirling and whirling as only a four-year-old can do. For a moment she was caught up again in the joy of what it had been like to be that free—before she'd known that there was any right or wrong way to do it. Before she had learned what it meant to be a Sheridan.

Suddenly, she smacked into something hard enough to rattle her teeth. A brick wall she was sure, but when she twisted around, all she saw was a broad, very large chest. Then Nick's hands were at her waist, pulling her close again.

"Are you okay?"

"Yes." Why was it, she wondered, that every time he pressed her close like this, the fit seemed more perfect, the need to stay more compelling?

"Try this," he suggested. And suddenly, it was so easy, with his hands at her waist to guide her, to give herself up to the music, to recapture the abandonment, the delight she'd known as a child.

The next time he pulled her close, he leaned down and spoke in her ear. "You're good at this. Are you sure you haven't been taking secret lessons?"

The compliment moved her, warmed her, and before

she could even think to reply, he continued, "Do you have any more hidden talents?"

Drawing back, she laughed up at him. "I think I'll surprise you."

"I'D FORGOTTEN what fresh air smells like," Tyler said as she drew in a deep breath and savored it. "Glorious."

"What did you say?" As he asked the question, Nick drew her farther along the sidewalk. The music pouring through the open door of the club was only a few decibels softer than it had been on the dance floor.

"The fresh air," Tyler said, surprised when the coolness on her skin made her shiver. "I didn't think I'd ever feel cool again."

Nick took the jacket he'd folded over his arm and draped it around her shoulders. She turned to him then. "I feel like this is a dream, and if I pinch myself, I'll wake up. I actually *danced*."

Nick grinned at her. "I'd say so. You wore me out, sugar."

Tyler cast a regretful glance back at the door of the club. The thrum of the bass was still vibrating beneath her feet. "And now it's back to reality. This must have been how Cinderella felt when she had to leave the ball at midnight." Drawing in another deep breath, she met Nick's eyes. "What do we do now?"

"We're back to planning, I see," he said as he laced his fingers through hers and began to walk toward the corner.

"It's the best way."

"Okay, how about this? There's a place I know about ten blocks from here. It's open all night and it serves the best breakfast in Manhattan. By the time we get there, we just might have our hearing back. And then you can tell me how you learned to dance like that."

She turned, pulling on his hand to stop him. "That's not—"

"Did you know your chin always lifts when you get annoyed?"

"It doesn't."

"It just did again."

Tyler's eyes narrowed. He was trying to distract her, and it would be very easy to let him succeed. But she couldn't. "Richard's kidnappers are going to get in touch with me sometime today, and when they do, they'll want a ransom. I can get some cash. My grandmother always made sure she kept a substantial amount of cash that she could get her hands on in a hurry. Then there's a banker I know who'll help me, depending on how much they ask for...I should contact him first thing..."

Nick's grip on her hand tightened. "You're not going to pay it."

"Of course, I am."

"And then what? Do you think it's going to be as simple as paying the money and they'll deliver your bridegroom back into your hands? Do you know how often paying a ransom succeeds in getting the victim back?"

A tiny sliver of ice shot up her spine. She'd forgotten how easily his eyes could go from laughter to fury. "No."

"Less then one percent of the cases."

Her throat went dry, but she stood toe to toe with him and met his eyes steadily. "I don't care what you think about Richard or whoever he is—I'm going to do whatever I can to save him. I want to make sure we're on the same page about that."

"The page we're on is a blank one." Nick bit out the words. "We don't know yet who's behind this or why. If we're lucky, one of Sam's operatives will start filling in some of those blanks soon. Until then—"

"Take your hands off the lady."

The gruff voice came from behind them, and when she turned Tyler recognized the two men who'd tried to snatch her in front of the Plaza. The one who looked like a linebacker had a large gun pointed at Nick. Fear lodged in her throat as she felt Nick's hand tighten briefly on hers before he released it.

"That's it. Now just keep your arms lifted out from your sides as you step away."

The moment he was a few feet away from her, the leaner of the two men moved toward her and clamped his hand around her arm. "Don't even think about screaming or we'll have to shoot your bodyguard right here."

"Move." The linebacker motioned Nick toward the mouth of an alley with his gun, and the man holding Tyler's arm fell into step behind his partner, drawing her with him.

It was a nightmare, Tyler thought as they marched in a strange parade into the dark alley. One that she and Nick might never wake up from. *Think.* Her mind seemed to be the only part of her that wasn't frozen with fear. The music from the club was growing fainter, the vibrations fading along with the fresh air. As the light from the street dimmed, the scent of rotting garbage grew stronger, along with the cloying, sweet smell of the aftershave of the man beside her.

"That's far enough," the linebacker said. "No one's going to hear us here."

In the shadowy dimness, Nick and the larger man

were barely more than silhouettes, but what light there was gleamed off the big man's gun. It was hard to breathe, Tyler discovered. She had to concentrate on pulling air in and letting it out. She had to fight against the weightlessness in her head.

"Put your hands against the wall and spread your legs. You know the drill," the linebacker growled. Once Nick had followed instructions, the man moved forward, holding the gun firmly against Nick's spine while feeling up and down his legs. When he found the revolver, he backed up, set it on the ground and kicked it away. Then, pocketing his own gun, he drove his fist into Nick's side. Nick sagged, turning as he did, but before he recovered, his opponent delivered two more blows.

Tyler lunged forward, but she got no farther than a step before the grip on her arm tightened and she was dragged roughly back. It was only when she felt the gun in Nick's jacket pocket slap into her thigh that she remembered it—the backup.

"Not so fast, sister. This'll only take Louie a minute. Then we're going to go for a little ride." The man holding her arm chuckled as his buddy delivered a punch to Nick's chin that sent him back against the brick wall of the building.

Tyler stood perfectly still, not even daring to breathe as she slipped her hand into the pocket and closed her fingers around the gun. In front of her, the linebacker moved in quickly to deliver another blow, and Nick crumpled, sliding down the wall. His opponent turned back to give a thumbs-up sign to his partner.

"Next time you hire a bodyguard, Louie and I are available," the man at her side said, chuckling again.

Suddenly Nick rose and launched himself into his

opponent. Together, they crashed to the ground, the big guy taking the brunt of the impact. Then they rolled together across the pavement.

Tyler prayed as she heard the crunch of fist against bone. Nick was on the bottom now, and he'd become a punching bag for Louie. She had to do something. Her fingers were slick with sweat as she tightened her grip on the gun and pulled it out. Aiming it away from the two men, she fired.

It was so loud. Her ears were ringing as the man holding her arm flung her away. Her head smacked hard into the wall, and stars swirled in front of her eyes. Blinking them away, she saw the man who'd held her barreling toward her, going for his gun. She raised hers with both hands and, praying that she wouldn't hit him, fired again.

"What the hell—" His gun clattered to the ground as he gripped his shoulder, then started backing away.

Out of the corner of her eye, she saw the one named Louie scramble to his feet. She pointed the barrel over his head and fired again. And again. And again.

In some part of her mind, she was aware that two men were racing away down the alley, but she couldn't seem to stop firing the gun. It wasn't loud anymore, just a series of clicks. Then Nick's hands were on hers, taking the weapon out of her hand and pulling her close.

For a moment all she could do was cling to him. "I was so afraid."

"Me, too," he murmured, running his hands over her, pressing her closer. "I was afraid to get up until I was sure you'd unloaded that thing."

"Stop," she said as she felt the bubble of laughter rise. If she let out the laugh, she wasn't sure she could stop. "It's not funny. I thought he was going to kill you."

"Yeah, I had the same thought about you." For a moment, the two of them just held on.

It was Nick who finally drew away. "We have to get out of here. They could decide to come back."

Tyler stared at him. There was blood dripping from his eyebrow and his lip. "You're hurt."

"Yeah," he said. "I think that jerk cracked one of my ribs. C'mon." Taking her hand, he walked back to pick up his other gun. "Why didn't you tell me you could shoot like that?"

She shook her head. "I can't. I was trying very hard to miss him."

Nick laughed then, and the sound of it melted away the rest of her fear. "You're a marvel, Tyler Sheridan."

NICK PACED BACK AND FORTH in the shadowy confines of his apartment. He would have preferred to be taking a five-mile run through the streets. That way he could quickly ease the anger that had been on a slow boil in his blood ever since he'd safely settled Tyler in the next room. And perhaps the jarring impact of the pavement each time his foot slammed down would have rid his mind of the image of Tyler being dragged down that alley in front of him. Pausing in front of the bedroom door, he eased it open, just enough to reassure himself that she was safe.

It was the third time he'd checked on her in the two hours since he'd laid her on the bed. He could barely make her out in the dim light filtering through the window. Moving closer, he saw that she lay curled on her side, one hand tucked under her cheek, her hair spread over the pillow. She'd fallen asleep in the taxi and had barely stirred when he'd carried her up the stairs. He hadn't dared to undress her, not even to remove his jacket. Her other hand was still clutching the lapel.

He'd brought her to his apartment because it seemed the safest place. Louie and his buddy undoubtedly knew that she was still registered at the Plaza. And he didn't want them to know where she was. Not until he figured out what part they were playing in the kidnapped bridegroom puzzle, and how they had tracked them to that dance club. That was what he couldn't figure out. He'd taken precautions ever since he'd almost lost her in front of the Plaza. Even as the fear rolled through him again, he moved closer to the bed, wanting to give in to an overwhelming urge to touch her. The truth was, he wanted to lie down on that bed beside her and just hold her.

But he couldn't indulge himself right now. He'd been careless. His mind had been too full of her as they'd left the dance club. He hadn't been thinking objectively. Once more the image of what might have been surfaced in his mind, bringing back the icy terror, the utter helplessness he'd felt when he'd heard that first shot ring out. For a second...that one eternal second between shots...he'd thought she was—

No. Frowning, he ran a hand through his hair as he stepped back from the bed. He couldn't afford to keep reliving that moment. He couldn't allow those feelings to cloud his mind and affect his judgment, either. Even the anger that had filled him since he'd gotten back to the apartment was preferable to the fear and the guilt.

As he watched her shoulder rise and fall with each breath she drew and released, he felt some of his tension ease. It occurred to him then that he'd spent a great deal of time since she'd first barged into his office fantasizing about getting her into his bed. And now that she was here, she was sleeping in it alone. His sense of humor erased more of the tension as he thought about it. The little ironies of life always amused him.

Turning, he walked quietly back into the living room and settled himself on the couch. It wasn't the only time Tyler Sheridan would sleep in his bed. And once he straightened out the mess she was in, she wouldn't be sleeping in it alone. On that thought, he fell immediately and deeply asleep.

NICK SAT STRAIGHT UP and listened hard. Something...some noise had jettisoned his mind from sleep to full consciousness. What? A quick glance around the room told him that he was alone. The locks on his door were good. Not a shadow was out of place. Rising, he moved to the window and silenced the rumble of the air conditioner.

Nothing. The illuminated dial of his watch told him that he'd slept barely an hour. Maybe it was just a delayed reaction to the events in that alley that was making him jumpy. He was halfway to the couch when he heard it—the whimpering sound of a child or an animal. Two strides took him into the bedroom, and he threw on the light.

Tyler lay curled into a tight little ball. The whimpering sounds were words. As he sat on the edge of the bed, he could just make out what she was saying.

"Stop...don't go!"

He touched her shoulder. "Tyler."

With a muffled scream, she jolted upright. Her eyes were unfocused and glazed with tears, huge ones spilling silently down her cheeks.

"It's okay, it's just a dream." He reached for her again, but she swatted at both of his hands. Then making a choked, desperate sound, she scooted away until her back was against the headboard of the bed.

"It's all right," he murmured in a soothing voice. The nightmare still held her captive. If he could just get her in his arms and hold her. "Tyler, it's me...Nick." He inched his way closer. "You're all right."

This time when he raised his hand, she bolted off the bed and streaked toward the door. Halfway through the living room, he grabbed her. Twisting in his arms, she stamped down hard enough on his foot to have him swearing under his breath. When he jerked her back against him, she slammed a fist into his ribs, the same ones that he was sure that bozo in the alley had cracked. Weakened for a moment by the pain shooting through him, he slackened his hold, and she raced toward the door.

While she struggled with a dead bolt, he drew in a deep breath, then winced. Maybe she'd done that bozo in the alley a favor by only winging him with the gun.

She was murmuring again, the words almost a chant. "Don't go. Don't go."

This time when he grabbed her, he immobilized her arms and dragged her back against his chest. Wrenching this way and that, she reawakened every bruise on his body. Then her foot connected with his shin, and he lunged into the wall, nearly toppling them both to the floor.

"Damn it, Tyler. It's—"

Her teeth sank into his arm and he yelped. "That tears it, sugar." Hoisting her off her feet, he shifted her against his good side and strode toward the bathroom.

He didn't want to hurt her. He didn't want her to hurt him. There was only one solution. Shoving the shower curtain aside, he stepped over the edge of the tub and turned the faucet. Icy water hit them full force.

Sputtering, Tyler stopped struggling and glared up at him. "What are you doing?"

"You had a nightmare." Her eyes were clear, the desperate look gone.

"I think I'm having another one right now. This water's freezing."

As the relief flooded through him, Nick struggled against a smile. "The better to wake you up with, my dear. You want the soap?"

Tyler frowned. "You've got to be kidding."

"Actually, I've got a plan. I know how much you like them. How about you scrub my back and I'll scrub yours?"

"We're fully dressed."

"Is that so?" He stepped back, setting her away from him. Then he raised both hands in surrender. "Okay, okay. If you insist, we'll strip. You first."

She had begun to shiver, her teeth were chattering. But she was standing now without his support, facing him. "I am not going to strip in the shower with you."

For a moment, he was tempted to prove her wrong, to show her how easy it would be. He'd accomplished what he'd wanted—to drive whatever horror she'd been trapped in out of her mind. But he'd spent most of the evening fantasizing about just how quickly he could have her out of that dress, naked and pressed against him. And then there would be another way that they could chase away the memory of that nightmare. Together.

The image that he'd conjured up became suddenly more vivid in his mind. As he watched a drop of water run down her cheek to her neck, he imagined what it would be like to follow its path with his mouth. He wanted a taste of her neck, he wanted to scrape his teeth against the vein that was throbbing there before sampling her shoulder, her ear. He wanted to run his soap-slicked hands over her shoulders, then down to her waist and lower. He clenched his hands into fists at his side to keep himself from reaching out. But he couldn't stop himself from imagining what it would be like. The drum of his own pulse roared in his ears, nearly drowning out the sound of the water. How easy it would be to slip his hands between her legs and enter her with one finger, and then two. To feel her close tightly around him.

Quite suddenly, he was no longer aware of the cold water. All he could feel was the heat that was within him. He raised his eyes to hers and saw that they'd darkened as if she, too, could picture exactly how it would be. Still, he didn't move.

He couldn't. He'd made a promise to himself. If he was going to protect her, he needed to keep some objectivity. She needed a PI right now more than she needed a lover.

"Okay." Reaching for the faucet, he cranked the water off and stepped out of the shower. After settling a towel around her shoulders, he said, "We'd better switch to the backup plan. You strip in here, and I'll strip in the bedroom. Then we'll both put on dry clothes and you'll tell me about your nightmare."

He made it to the door without looking back. Then he glanced over his shoulder. She was still standing there, looking at him. Two strides would take him back to her.

"Damn." He swore under his breath as he closed the door on her. This was a perfect example of why he really hated plans.

8

TYLER STARED at the closed bathroom door and fought against the urge to run after Nick, to stop him. She'd taken two steps and was reaching for the knob when she jerked her hand back. What was the matter with her? She never acted on impulse. She had to think first, weigh the pros and cons. Turning, she glanced at her reflection in the mirror. The woman staring back at her was someone she barely recognized. Her wet hair was plastered to the sides of her face, her cheeks were flushed.

The woman's eyes were different, too. There was a hint of recklessness she'd never seen before. Certainly, she'd never allowed herself to act on it before. What if she did right now?

Tyler drew in a deep breath and let it out. Then she turned toward the door. He'd said he was going to change his clothes. He could be standing naked in the middle of his bedroom this moment. She could easily come up with a plan to handle that. All she had to was walk through that door. What was stopping her? She wanted him. He wanted her.

Her fingers were closing around the doorknob when it suddenly struck her. Confusion shot through her even as the knowledge filled her mind.

She was falling in love with Nick Romano. Backing

quickly away from the door, she sank down on the edge of the bathtub.

The whole idea was impossible. His future was in California. Hers was in Boston. What kind of a plan was going to handle that?

It would have to be a pretty damn good one, she thought. Straightening her shoulders, she stood up. She was a CEO, wasn't she? Plans were her life.

The knock on the door made her jump.

"Hey, I could use some help out here. Cooking is not one of my talents."

"I'll be right out," Tyler said.

"I left some clothes for you on the bed."

She walked to the door and, after drawing in a deep breath, turned the handle. Every good plan began with Step One, and she knew what that would be.

But when she stepped into the bedroom, it was empty, and the door to the living room was shut. Not sure whether it was relief or disappointment she felt at the reprieve, she walked to the bed. The shirt he'd laid out was one of his. It was blue chambray, soft with many washings. The moment she slipped into it, she caught his scent. She was rolling the sleeves up when she noticed the other clothes he'd laid out for her. The jeans definitely did not belong to him. They were much too small, and might even fit her, she thought. And then she saw the briefs, white and edged with lace. The jealousy hit first, twisting sharply before the anger bubbled up. Whirling, she stormed out of the bedroom.

"Just what do you think you're doing?" she asked.

A cracked eggshell in one hand, Nick turned to face her across the narrow counter. "I'm trying to feed you. And it's not going well."

Through the red haze of her anger, she could see several bowls littering the once clean counter, and smoke rising out of a pan on the stove.

"This is the second frying pan I've scorched," he explained as he grabbed the handle, then swore and shook his hand. "And I keep getting shells in with the eggs. I've never cooked for a woman before in my life."

Tyler fisted her hands on her hips. "No, I imagine you kept your previous lady friends otherwise engaged in the shower."

"What are you talking about?" Nick asked as he made a second attempt to grab the smoking pot, this time protecting his hand with a towel.

"I'm talking about the other women you've entertained in this apartment," Tyler said as she rounded the end of the counter and joined him in the cramped kitchen space.

"I haven't—damn!" The pan dropped with a clatter into the sink. The moment he turned the faucet on, it hissed and spat steam at him.

She poked him in the back to get his attention. "And then, of course, they were probably all too willing to whip you up something in the kitchen. Well, I've got news for you."

Nick turned to face her. "That might be very helpful since I don't have any idea what you're ranting about."

Tyler folded her arms across her chest. "I don't cook, either."

Drawing in a deep breath, Nick ran his hands through his hair. Behind him, the skillet gave one final hiss before it lost its battle with the water. "Look, I don't think I'm following the thread of this conversation. Suppose you start over and tell me why you're so upset."

"I'm not going to wear some other woman's jeans."

"You're not..." Suddenly, the frown on his face cleared. "You're upset because of the jeans?"

"I won't wear them. And I won't wear the panties, either."

She could have sworn the corners of his lips twitched, but his voice was serious when he said, "Let me see if I've got this straight. You're upset about the jeans because you think they belong to some woman friend. In other words, you're jealous."

"I'm not..." Pausing, she lifted her chin. "Well, what if I am?"

This time the corners of his lips definitely twitched. She dropped her hands and clenched them into fists.

Nick raised his hands, palms out. "Truce. My ribs can't take another punch. The jeans belong to Grace."

"They do?"

"Scout's honor. I told you my sisters sleep over sometimes. They also leave clothes here just in case they decide to come on the spur of the moment. I thought Grace's might fit you."

"Oh. I thought..." Tyler felt her cheeks burn. "I'm sorry."

He studied her for a moment. "And I didn't keep you *otherwise engaged* in the shower because I'm losing my objectivity where you're concerned. What happened in the alley tonight was my fault."

"No." Tyler shook her head. "It wasn't. I don't want you to think that."

"It's my job to protect you, and I wasn't thinking about that. I was thinking about you. So I've come up with a plan. Step One is you're going back into the bedroom and put Grace's clothes on while I give these eggs another try," Nick said.

She watched him turn away, pick up an egg and

crack it on the edge of the bowl. Then she said, "I want you to finish what you wanted to do in the shower."

When he dropped both the shell and the egg into the bowl, she felt her confidence inch up a little. But his voice was cool, his tone steady when he turned to face her. "I suppose CEOs are used to giving orders, but I don't take them very well."

"Okay," she said in a reasonable tone. Then she began to unbutton her shirt.

"Don't do that," Nick warned.

"My plan didn't work, so I'm improvising," she explained.

He grabbed the edges of the shirt just as she slipped the last button free. "Tyler—"

She met his eyes steadily. "I've spent my whole life planning and living for the future. I want to make love to you right here and now."

He didn't say a thing, didn't move.

"Don't you want me?" she asked.

Releasing the breath he'd been holding, Nick curled his fingers more tightly into the shirt and drew her closer. For a moment he rested his forehead against hers. "I've wanted you from the moment I jumped off that couch and saw you standing in my office."

"Then let me take this shirt off."

Lifting his head, he said, "You have to be sure."

Looking into his eyes, she glimpsed his own uncertainty. It was the first time she'd seen any chink in the self-confidence that radiated from his very core. She touched him then, running one hand up his chest and neck to rest against his cheek. "Let me show you how sure I am," she murmured, as she used only the slightest pressure to draw his face closer and closer until finally she could press her lips to his. The simple pleasure of the feelings moving through her reminded her again of coming home, not to a place she'd ever been, but to a place she'd always dreamed of. Slowly, she moved her mouth on his, pressing, then sampling, eager to explore each taste, each change in texture.

"Touch me, please," she whispered against his lips.

He did, raising his hands to her face. She felt his fingers spread, then skim along her jawline, her cheekbones, her temples, until they finally came to rest in her hair.

"More," she whispered.

His hands didn't move. Only his mouth did, to nip at her lower lip. Then, when she thought she would die from the wanting, his tongue touched hers and he began to sample her slowly and thoroughly. A ribbon of pleasure unwound through her right down to her toes. Through the thin fabric of the shirt, she could feel his heat, and her bare skin burned where it was pressed fully against his. Her breasts tightened against his chest and her lower body yielded to his hardness.

Still his hands remained tangled in her hair, and he made love to her with his mouth alone. The room was quiet; the only sound was her sigh as his lips moved down the curve of her neck. She could feel her blood thicken, her muscles grow lax. It seemed she had waited all her life for this. For Nick. A quick tease from his teeth, a flick of his tongue along her collarbone, had her whispering, "Please. Touch me."

As he slipped the shirt off her shoulders, then ran his hand down her back and over her hip, a thousand little needs sprang up to pulse beneath every inch of her skin.

"More."

"What would you like me to do?" His voice was a whisper in her ear.

"What you were thinking of doing in the shower."

Drawing back, he smiled then, slowly. "That would be my pleasure." Then gripping her waist with both hands, he lifted her onto the counter. "First, I was going to rub you all over with soap." He began to touch her then, exactly the way he'd fantasized doing it, skimming his fingers in a slow journey over her shoulders, down her arms. Her skin was even softer than he'd imagined, as delicate to the touch as fine porcelain. He felt it warm as he traced a path back to her shoulders. To torture them both, he settled his hands at her waist, then drew them up her sides until his palms were resting beneath her breasts. Slowly, with his eyes on hers, he rubbed his thumbs over her nipples, and when her breath caught in her throat, he rubbed them back again. The shudder that moved through her ignited a response deep within him, and he had to push down the urge to hurry.

"Nick..."

"I've been thinking about doing this for so long," he murmured, flattening his palms as she arched into his hands. Nothing in his fantasies had come close to the reality of seeing her eyes darken with delight, of hearing her breathe his name with such desperation. Even with the need drumming through him, he had to have more. Skimming his hand over her stomach, he stroked his fingers down her inner thigh. Her skin was even softer there, and satin smooth. As he watched her breath catch and shudder out, desire twisted into an ache inside him. He could picture how easy it would be to grip her hips and slide her forward to the edge of the counter. Then all he would have to do was unsnap and lower his jeans

and he could be inside her. That was what he'd fantasized doing to her in the shower. Taking her before either one of them had a chance to think. But now, what
he wanted more than anything was to give her more.
When her head dropped back, he leaned forward to
close his mouth over her breast.

As the sweetness streamed through him, the hold he
had on his control began to loosen. Sweeping his
tongue across her nipple, he savored the subtle change
in flavor as she arched closer and moaned his name. He
could feel her nails digging into his shoulder, her pulse
hammering beneath his lips, urging him.

"Nick...please."

When he slipped his fingers into her, she arched back
immediately, her body shuddering in climax.

"Incredible," he murmured as he drew her close and
cradled her head against his chest. "It drives me crazy
to be able to touch you and make you mine."

His words were only a rumble in her ear. She
couldn't seem to separate them. She didn't need to. For
the moment, all she wanted was to hold him, to hold on
to the moment. The only thought in her mind was that
as long as she could, he was hers.

Nick moved first, drawing her head back to kiss her
softly. His mouth was gentle, his lips light as a feather
as they brushed over hers. Then slowly, deliberately, he
deepened the kiss until she could taste the desire, hot
and ripe, and feel the instant race of his heart beneath
her hand. She'd thought it would be impossible to feel
anything again so quickly, but waves of pleasure swept
through her. When she drew back, what she saw in his
eyes kindled a fire inside her all over again. Moving her
hands to his shoulders, she said, "I think it's my turn to
show you what I wanted to do to *you* in the shower."

"Be my guest," Nick said.

She slipped off the counter to stand before him. Then slowly, she drew her fingers down his chest, pausing when they were resting lightly against his nipples. His quick intake of breath increased the heat that was steadily building in her center. Testing herself and him, she circled his nipples once, then again. "Actually, I wanted to do this the first time I saw you asleep on the couch in your office."

His eyes narrowed even as they grew darker, more intent on hers. "You did?"

"I wanted to do more," she murmured, drawing her fingers down to his stomach, pleased at the quick contraction of his muscles. His skin was so smooth, so hard. She flattened her palms against him just above the waistband of his jeans; then, using her mouth, she began to retrace the journey her fingers had just taken. "I wanted to do this," she breathed against him as she slowly circled his nipple with her tongue. "And this," she whispered as she switched her attention to the other side. When he moaned her name, she could feel it, taste it. The flavor wound through her like a drug. *Slowly, slowly*, she reminded herself as she moved her lips lower and lower until they reached the barrier of his jeans. Then she drew back.

"I wanted to do this, too," she said. Her voice sounded husky, breathless as she slipped her fingers beneath his waistband and pulled at the snap. His eyes were on hers as she drew down the zipper, then tugged at his jeans until they slid to the floor. He wore nothing beneath, and he was magnificent. Without any hesitation, she reached out and curled her fingers around him, savoring the sensation of hardness encased in velvet.

He drew in a quick harsh breath. "Don't move. Not for a moment."

She didn't think she could have, even if she'd wanted to. All she knew was that she wanted him with a need so great that she was sure she would shatter from it. Then his hand was on hers, gently closing around her fingers and drawing them away.

"Here, let me do this while I still can," he said as he released her hand to draw a foil-wrapped packet out of his pocket. He fumbled a little as he ripped it open, then finally sheathed himself.

"I'm not sure I would have managed this quite so well in the shower. I know I wouldn't have given you time to touch me. I would have done this—" His mouth crushed hers, his taste desperate. But he gave her no time to savor it. In a move that made her head spin, he had her on the floor. His fingers dug hard into her as he positioned her on top of him, straddling his hips. Then lifting her as if she were weightless, he lowered her slowly, inch by inch, until he filled her.

Go slowly. The words drummed in his mind, growing fainter as her softness closed around him, and the thin grasp he had on his control slipped away. He turned them both so that she was beneath him on the floor. Desire became a white hot flash, searing through him, pushing him to thrust into her again and again until need became delirium. In some dim part of his mind, he was aware that she was moving, too, matching her rhythm perfectly with his, faster and faster, higher and higher, until the speed catapulted them both into an explosion of pleasure.

WHEN HE COULD THINK AGAIN, breathe again, he was lying on top of her on the kitchen floor, her hand fisted on his chest as tightly as his was in her hair. As if they were both determined to hold onto the moment. He wasn't sure he could move even if he wanted to. No other woman had drained his energy or his control this way. Had he hurt her? He certainly had to be doing serious damage right now. The thought gave him the strength to lever himself up.

"Don't go." Her hand gripped his shoulder.

"I'm crushing you," he said.

"I don't care," she said, wrapping both arms around him. "I don't want you to go."

"Then I'll take you with me," he said, sitting up and lifting her onto his lap. "Better?"

"Mmm," she murmured as she settled her head on his shoulder. "I don't think we could have done all that in the shower."

"We could always put your theory to the test."

He felt her lips curve in a smile against him. Then, for a while, they sat in silence, saying nothing. It occurred to Nick that he could have gone on sitting just like that, naked on the kitchen floor with Tyler on his lap, for a very long time. But he'd had a plan when he'd left her in the bathroom, and her words to him had brought it back.

"'Don't go.' That's what you kept saying in your nightmare. Tell me about it."

She stiffened in his arms. He merely tightened his hold on her.

"Tell me," he said again.

Tyler shook her head. "It's silly really. I haven't had it in years. It must have been shooting the gun that triggered it."

He pushed her hair back from her face, running his fingers through it. "What's it about?"

She glanced up at him. "Is this how you interrogate your suspects?"

His brows lifted. "*Interrogate?* That's what cops do. We PI's have to be more subtle." He paused and let the silence stretch. "We're dogged and determined, dedicated and devilishly clever."

"And dreadfully pushy," she added.

He smiled at her then. "You got that right, sugar. C'mon. I couldn't get you to wake up. It can't do anything but help if you talk about it."

With a sigh, she laid her head back on his shoulder. "It's always about the night my father died. It's dark and I'm cold. The voices wake me up. They're so angry. But I can't make out the words. I get out of my bed and sneak to the top of the stairs. Through the spindles in the railing, I can see down into the foyer. The light from the parlor is splashing across it in a wide band, and I can see long shadows. One of them is still and the other is moving. I can recognize the voices now. It's my father and my mother, and they're arguing."

Nick felt the first tear and then the second as they ran down her cheek and dripped onto his shoulder. Living in a house full of women, he had long ago schooled himself to deal with them. Brushing his lips against her temple, he simply held her.

"And then suddenly there's silence. I can only hear the footsteps coming closer, one of the shadows shortening and growing clearer. When he strides into the foyer, I can see it's my father. He grabs his coat and heads to the door. I want to call out to him, *Don't go.* I reach my hands through the spindles and I can feel my lips forming the words. But no sound comes out. And he leaves. It's only when the door slams behind him that I can say the words so that I can hear them. But it's too late. He's gone."

Her face was hot, her cheeks drenched, her body shuddering with her silent sobs as he continued to hold her close and stroke her hair. Finally, when he could tell that her tears were spent, he said, "And that was the night your father died?"

Tyler nodded against his shoulder. "The roads were slick, and our house sat on a hill outside Boston. The police said he lost control of the car and it crashed through a guardrail."

Nick gripped her shoulders and turned her to face him. "He wouldn't have stopped even if you had called out. It wasn't your fault."

"I know that. I really do. It's just...haven't you ever wished that you could go back and change one thing...that maybe things could have been different?"

"Yes. But you can't."

She studied him for a moment, caught by his tone. "What would you like to change?"

He ran a hand down her back. "I'd like to change that the first time we made love, we did it on the kitchen floor."

Tyler smiled at him. "I wouldn't change that. And I don't think that's what you were thinking of."

Nick was saved from a reply when his stomach growled. "You must be hungry," he said immediately.

"Me? That was *your* stomach."

Nick glanced down. "Really?" Then he looked at her again. "You know, I have a confession to make. I can't cook."

Tyler's eyes narrowed. "I might have fallen for that one if I hadn't seen the cookbook and all those cooking show tapes on your bookshelf."

Nick grinned at her. "Snooping? I didn't think Sheridans did that."

"Don't change the subject. Why all the tapes if you don't cook? And why have eggs if you can't do anything with them?"

Nick leaned back against the cupboard and grinned at her. "You were curious about me. Admit it."

Her chin lifted. "Maybe a little."

Leaning forward, he kissed her nose. "It's only a short way from curiosity to fascination."

Her brow rose. "Really?"

"See where it's led already?"

"I'm naked and starving on the kitchen floor," she pointed out, then added, "'Fess up. Why do you have eggs if you don't know how to cook them?"

"Lucy brought them the other night. She makes a mean omelette."

"And the books and tapes?"

"It's a tradition in the Romano family for all of the men to cook. I don't. However, hope springs eternal in the hearts of my family. The tapes and the books are their way of encouraging me to learn."

"Why don't you?" Tyler asked.

Nick shrugged. "Rebellion, I guess. My father tried to teach me, but I wasn't an apt pupil. I never did anything right."

Tyler studied him for a moment. There wasn't a trace of emotion in his voice, but she could tell he was talking about more than cooking. And she knew about the pain that came from never being able to measure up to expectations. "Wasn't he happy with your other accomplishments?"

"Lord no," Nick said. "He hated the fact that I wanted to go to law school. He wanted me to follow in his footsteps and become a cop. I knew I'd never please him doing that, either. We were fighting about it the night he died."

"I'm sorry." Not sure what to say, she put her arms around him then and simply held him.

"Even if I could go back and change that night," he said, "I'm not sure it would make any difference. I was eighteen. We were fighting a lot. Lawyers weren't as unpopular then as they are now, but he'd seen one too many crooks get off because they had a fancy 'mouthpiece.' If he'd lived, I'm not sure he ever would have understood."

Nick's stomach growled again.

She held him for a moment longer before she drew away. "I think we're going to starve."

He sighed. "Well, we do have that cookbook. You're a top flight CEO and I'm a phenomenal PI. Maybe we should work together on this."

"Equal partners," Tyler bargained as she extended her hand.

"Deal," Nick said.

"IT DOESN'T LOOK HALF BAD," Tyler said as she divided the eggs evenly between Nick's plate and her own.

"Those shells I dropped in will only give a little added crunch," Nick said, taking the plates and setting them on the counter.

"Shells?" Tyler asked pointedly. She climbed onto a stool and gave the eggs a dubious look. "Your job was to get them out."

Nick spooned instant coffee into a mug and filled it with water he'd boiled. "I don't think partners should criticize each other." Then, sitting down next to her, he sampled the eggs. "These are actually good."

Tyler tried hers, then said, "By George, maybe we've got it."

Nick grinned at her around another mouthful. It had taken them over an hour to make breakfast. Before they'd tackled the project, she'd wanted to take a shower, and this time he'd joined her. The hot water had run out long before they'd explored all of his earlier fantasy. But neither of them had been cold, not even with the icy water pouring down. Just the memory had his body tightening again. She'd put on one of his shirts and Grace's jeans, and with her hair pulled back in a ponytail, she didn't look much older than his kid sister. One strand of her hair had fallen loose, and he had to keep his hands tight on his mug to prevent himself from reaching out and tucking it behind her ear. Because he wasn't sure he could stop with one touch.

Lifting his mug of coffee, he took a sip. He wanted to make love with her again right now. And he could. All he had to do was touch her. Mentally he shook his head. What kind of a spell had she put on him? He should be sated. The desire that had been building steadily within him since he'd first met her should have diminished, not increased.

Just then, she raised her eyes to meet his, and it struck him with the force of a Mack truck. He was in love with her.

"What's wrong?" she asked.

If he told her, she'd probably turn and run. She'd wanted what they could have in the present, the now. But there was no place in her future for Nick Romano...unless he could come up with a plan to convince her otherwise.

"Tell me," she said.

"We make pretty good partners," he said.

Her smile bloomed slowly. "We didn't starve. But I'm not sure we should push our luck. Scrambled eggs are pretty simple."

He set his mug down and propped his elbows on the counter. "Have you ever wanted to do something other than run Sheridan Trust?"

"When I was five, I wanted to be a ballet dancer."

"What changed your mind?"

"Madame Sobieski. I studied with her until I was twelve, when she told me I'd never have the body of a dancer. I needed longer arms and legs, a slimmer torso, a more graceful neck."

"I like your body just fine. Were you terribly disappointed?"

Tyler shook her head. "I wasn't really thinking of pursuing it as a career by then. I already pretty much had my sights set on running Sheridan Trust."

"To please your grandmother?"

She frowned a little. "Not entirely, although I very much wanted to prove to her that I was up to the task. But it was a business my father loved. He used to talk to me about it even when I was small. About how much joy it gave him to make money for his investors and for the stockholders through his decisions. That's why I want to close this deal with Bradshaw Enterprises. We'll be able to create new companies." Pushing her plate away, she leaned her elbows on the counter. "What about you? Have you always wanted to be a lawyer?"

He shot her a grin. "Ever since the first time I watched a Perry Mason rerun. I even hunted down and collected all the Erle Stanley Gardner books."

"Perry Mason didn't just get his clients off. He also

caught the bad guys. I'll bet that's what you liked about him."

"That and the fact that he had a great secretary. I always used to wonder where Perry and Della Street did it after hours."

She was laughing as she shook her head. "You're incorrigible."

He shrugged. "I was fourteen. Sex was on my mind a lot."

When she merely looked at him and raised her brows, he laughed, taking one of her hands and lifting it to his lips. "Trust me. I don't think of it nearly as much now."

"Why did you become a PI?"

He kept her hand in his. "After my father died, I had to postpone college and law school. If I couldn't be Perry Mason, I figured I could settle for Paul Drake."

Tilting her head, she studied him for a minute. "That way you could still get the bad guys."

"It had a lot more to do with getting an instant job I could be good at. Being a good PI boils down to solving puzzles. I've always been good at that."

"Crossword puzzles," she said.

"Snooping again?"

"It would have been hard to miss them. I do them, too."

He stared at her for a minute, then murmured, "And they said we had nothing in common."

For a moment they merely looked at one another. He could see in her eyes a reflection of the same curiosity and surprise he was feeling. It was Tyler who finally broke the silence.

"How is detective work like a crossword puzzle?"

"They both take a lot of patience, and in the end it's

usually a matter of feeding all the information you've gathered into a bunch of little slots—like the squares you put those letters in. Every last piece has to fit. One letter left over and you have to find another word—or culprit."

She sighed. "What happens when you have a case where nothing fits into the squares?"

Understanding the meaning behind her question, he replied, "We wait until we uncover more information. We're going to meet Sam at his office at ten o'clock, and that ought to help."

The shrill ring of the cell phone had Nick moving to the coffee table where he'd tossed it earlier. "Who do you think it is?"

She drew in a deep breath and let it out. "Naomi or Howard. And I'm running out of excuses about Richard."

Grinning at her, he handed her the phone. "You'll think of something."

"Hello...Mother?"

Nick watched with interest as she sank right down on the coffee table. All of the energy she'd had seconds ago seemed to be streaming away.

"Did Howard ask you to call me?"

The change in her tone of voice from surprise to frost, and the whitening of her knuckles on the phone, told him a great deal about her relationship with her mother.

"No, I can't meet you for lunch. I'm not sure yet what Richard's plans are.... Of course, everything's fine. Look, I have to go now. I'll talk to you later. 'Bye." She stared for a moment at the phone before she raised her eyes to meet Nick's. "My mother never calls me. I didn't even think she had this number."

Nick frowned suddenly. "Who would she get it from?"

"From Howard. She flew in with him last night. They're at the Plaza." Suddenly, she frowned.

"What is it?"

"That wasn't where Howard called from last night. When he asked me to call him back because of the static, it wasn't the number of the Plaza that I dialed. And the call didn't go through a switchboard."

"Do you remember the number you called him at last night?"

"No."

"Let me see the phone," he said. The moment she handed it to him, he checked the caller ID. "It's still there," he said as he punched in the numbers.

On the third ring, a recorded voice answered and began to issue instructions.

"It's not a hotel. It's some kind of voice-mail system," Nick said.

"Last night, whoever answered put me right through to Howard."

"Damn," Nick said as he cut the connection and checked his watch. "I'll bet that's how they found us last night. They had you call back and then they traced the call to the general area we were in."

"They can trace a cell phone?"

"With the right equipment. And I just gave them time to do it again."

Moving quickly to the window, he glanced down at the street. It was clear...for the moment.

"You're wrong. I can't believe that Howard could be involved in this."

Turning, he walked back and drew her to her feet. "This isn't the time to try to fit the pieces into the squares. Right now we have to move fast."

9

BEFORE THEY LEFT his apartment, Nick had insisted they don makeshift disguises. In spite of their hurry, Tyler barely recognized her reflection in the window at the end of the hallway. With her hair stuffed into one of Nick's old baseball caps, she looked like a boy. In the frayed flannel shirt he'd slipped on to camouflage his guns, Nick looked ready to join the ranks of the homeless. As he unlatched and raised the window, both of their images disappeared.

"You first," he said, gesturing her through the opening.

"We're going down the fire escape?"

"If I'm right and they traced us through your cell phone, they could be here at any minute. I'm not in the mood to stroll down any more alleys."

"I still don't think you're right. It just doesn't make sense. Why would Howard be involved in kidnapping Richard?"

"If I'm wrong, you can dock my fee. Right now, I don't want to take any chances. Hurry."

Against her better judgment, Tyler swung her leg over the sill. The minute she shifted her full weight onto the fire escape, it creaked ominously.

"Don't worry," Nick said. "It was inspected recently. Just don't look down."

"Now you tell me," she muttered as she tore her gaze

off the concrete pavement six stories below and waited
for a wave of dizziness to pass. Staring straight ahead,
she cautiously began her descent. A series of rattles and
groans joined in a little symphony with the creaks, and
when she reached the first landing, the whole fire escape seemed to sway. She made a grab for the railing,
then felt her heart lodge in her throat when it moved
outward.

"I wouldn't lean too much of my weight against that,
just in case," Nick warned.

"Right," she muttered, jerking her hand back to her
side. "Did I forget to tell you that I don't like heights?"

She felt his hands grip her shoulders and squeeze
them briefly. "You're doing great. Just take it one step
at a time."

She concentrated on keeping her balance. At the bottom of the next flight, she reminded herself to breathe.
After that, it seemed to get easier. She was beginning to
feel as if she was on a roll, when she reached the final
landing and stopped short. It was a good fifteen-foot
drop to the ground.

"Where's the ladder?" she asked.

"The tenants insisted it be removed," Nick explained.
"They were worried about break-ins. We can jump
down. But it would be another matter to jump up this
distance."

"Jump down? You've got to be kidding! I can't."

"Sure you can, sugar. Just watch." He lowered himself over the edge, then hung by his hands for a moment
before he made the drop. She winced when she heard
the impact of his feet hitting the cement and his accom-
panying grunt. A second later he was smiling up at her,
arms outstretched. "C'mon, I'll catch you."

For a moment, she hesitated. The only alternative

was to climb back up the fire escape. As she dropped to her hands and knees, she tried not to think of the distance she would be dropping. Instead, she concentrated on the gritty feel of the rust beneath her palms as she turned and lowered her legs over the edge. Then, bracing her weight on her forearms, she inched her way backward. The edge of the platform felt warm as she gripped it and let the force of gravity pull at her until she was hanging by her hands.

"I'll catch you," Nick called up from below.

Blocking out every thought but that, she let go. It took only seconds, but she was sure her heart and several other organs shot upward to lodge in her throat before her body crashed into Nick's. Arms, strong as iron, clamped around her as they both flew backward onto the cement.

She lay still for a moment, winded, stunned. Then she said, "That was actually fun."

"Speak for yourself, sugar," Nick grunted out, as he relaxed his arms and rolled her off him.

Scrambling to her feet, she grabbed his hand and helped him up. "Are you sure you're supposed to fall down like that when you catch somebody?"

Gripping her chin, he gave her a quick kiss. "You're never supposed to criticize your partner, especially when you've just squashed him like a bug." Quickly darting a glance in both directions, he pulled her with him to the nearest end of the alley.

"Stay back," he ordered as he flattened himself against the brick wall of the building and slowly inched his way to the corner. He risked one quick look. The street was clear except for a florist's van parked directly across the street. A man was struggling to drag a potted tree down the ramp that extended out the back doors.

Nick was about to turn back to Tyler and give her the all-clear signal when he recognized the black, windowless van turning the corner.

"Damn. They're here," he said as he glanced around. "Quick. The Dumpster." Grabbing her arm, he shoved her toward it. They barely had a chance to dive behind it before he heard the van rev its motor as it turned into the alley.

Slipping his gun out of the holster, he glanced at Tyler. The shock on her face had him leaning closer. "Don't fall apart on me now," he whispered.

"You were right. Howard must be involved...."

With his free hand, he gripped her arm. "Shh. Don't think about that. Just concentrate on the next few minutes. Can you do that?"

When she nodded, he drew back. The van was so close, he could hear the crunch of dirt and broken glass beneath its tires. His mind began to race. If one of them decided to get out and search more closely, he'd have to create a diversion so Tyler could run. Leaning close to her, he whispered, "When I tell you, I want you to run into the building across the street. The door is open for a delivery. Understand?"

At her nod, he let out the breath he was holding, and then they waited. The seconds seemed to stretch endlessly as they listened to the van move slowly past them. Then just as slowly, the noise of the engine grew fainter. Nick fought against the urge to risk a quick look until the sound had faded away completely. When he peered around the corner of the Dumpster, the alley was clear.

"They'll keep circling. We haven't got much time. Once we get to the end of the alley, we'll split up. I'll run toward the front of the building and distract them.

You race in the opposite direction and take the first taxi you can find. I'll meet you at Sam's office."

"I've got a better idea," Tyler said. "We're going to hitch a ride in that florist's van that's parked in the street. C'mon."

She was out from behind the Dumpster before he could stop her. He sprinted after her, catching up at the end of the alley. The street was clear, and so was the ramp leading into the florist's van. Together they raced toward it, and seconds later they were hunkered down behind a jungle of potted plants.

The moment he caught his breath, he grabbed Tyler by the shoulders and turned her toward him. There wasn't a trace of fear in her eyes.

"Okay, what's next?" she asked.

The laugh started low within him, and he had to struggle to keep it from bursting free. One thing he knew for sure. If he hadn't already taken that long leap into love with her, he'd be doing it right now.

"Tyler Sheridan, you're a marvel," he said as he drew her close and covered her mouth with his.

TYLER GOT HER FIRST LOOK at Sam Romano's office through a sea of green fern. At Nick's insistence, she'd paid the driver of the delivery van fifty dollars so they could carry plants into the high-rise that housed Sam's security firm. "It was a precaution," Nick had explained, just in case the goons in the windowless, black van had followed them. She hadn't argued. After all, she would have paid the driver twice that amount just for taking them there. But he'd cooperated fully once he'd seen the fake police badge Nick had shown him.

Sam was sitting behind his desk poring over some papers when Nick opened the door. After one puzzled glance, his face broke into a wide grin. "I feel like I'm in the last act of *Macbeth* and Birnham Wood is arriving at Dunsinane."

"You'll have to pardon my cousin," Nick said as he plunked his potted palm down in a corner. "He's highly literate."

Sam rose, took the fern out of her hands and placed it near the window. "It's all Nick's fault. He was always reading Shakespeare aloud during those long, boring stakeouts we used to go on, and some of it sank in. Sit down. I can't wait to hear why you're bringing me plants."

"We had to hitch a ride in a florist's delivery van," Nick said. "The two men who tried to snatch Tyler in front of the Plaza yesterday made another attempt last night when we came out of a dance club. Then they showed up at my apartment this morning. I think they're tracing her on her cell phone. Both times we called a certain number before they showed up." As Nick rattled the number off, Sam jotted it down.

"I'll see what I can do," Sam said. "Since it's a weekend, it'll take a little longer. When you called, who did you speak to?"

"The first time, it was my stepfather, Howard Tremaine," Tyler said, trying to ignore the tightness that settled in her chest.

"But there was static," Nick added. "Can you be one-hundred-percent certain it was him?"

Tyler shook her head slowly. "No, but maybe that's just wishful thinking."

"Try to keep your feelings out of it," Nick said. "Good detective work depends on being totally objective. Right, Sam?"

"That's the key. Why don't the two of you run

through what you've got so far—bounce your theories and suspicions off me."

Nick grinned at him. "I was hoping you'd ask. It all started with a Dear John letter Tyler received in the Personals a week before her wedding."

Sam glanced from Nick to Tyler. "That's an odd beginning."

"Then a ransom note arrives, and it appears that her bridegroom is kidnapped. But Tyler and I are beginning to think that more is going on than a simple kidnapping."

Tyler and I. Tyler wondered at the simple pleasure the words brought, as Nick continued to review what had happened so far. *Tyler and I.* She liked the sound of it. It made them sound like a couple...which in an odd kind of way they were. Both of them were out of place in Sam's sleek chrome-and-glass office. In their ragged clothes, they offered a sharp contrast to Sam's neat business suit. And during the climb down the fire escape and the dash to the florist's van, they'd worked well as a team. Suddenly, she became aware that both men were looking at her expectantly.

"What?" she asked.

"Sam was remarking on how efficient the Dear John letter in the personals was in so many ways. First, it gives the impression that it could only be from Richard. Second, whoever sent it can bank on the fact that you'll mention it to no one until you check it out. No one wants it to get out that they've been jilted. Finally, it brings you immediately to New York and away from your family and the business."

"So you're alone and vulnerable when you get the ransom note," Sam added. "Very clever."

"Except she hires me," Nick said. "That was probably not anticipated."

Tyler looked from one man to the other. "Maybe that's why those two men in the van are so anxious to take me for a ride. Maybe they want to get me away from Nick."

Grinning from ear to ear, Nick looked at Sam. "She really is good, isn't she?"

Nodding, Sam turned to Tyler. "If you ever want to take a break from being a CEO, I could get you a job here."

"But that still doesn't tell us why," Tyler said.

"Money," Sam said. "Or passion. Do you have any old boyfriends who don't want you to get married?"

"No," Tyler said.

"Then it's money. It usually is."

"And maybe more than the ransom is involved," Nick said as he began to pace. "If that was Howard on the phone last night, this could all be part of a plot to undermine Tyler's credibility at Sheridan Trust." Turning to Tyler, he asked, "If the board asked you to step down, who would they appoint as temporary CEO?"

"If I had to guess, I'd say Howard. With the Bradshaw deal hanging in the balance, they'd want to preserve the image of a family-run company for a while."

"He'd have a lot of power during the transition. And if Howard and this fake Richard were working together, it might explain how your bridegroom managed to squeeze through a security check."

Tyler gripped her hands tightly together as she pictured piece after piece of the puzzle slipping into little squares.

"I'm still curious as to when this little plot was hatched," Nick said as he paused and resumed his seat on the edge of Sam's desk. "And how that Internet dating service is connected. Did Howard know that you were using them?"

With a sigh, Tyler nodded. "I told him when I had our security run a check on them."

"Did anyone else know besides your friend Stevie?" Nick asked.

"My assistant Naomi Prescott knew. She came into my office one day when I was looking through the questionnaire. She mentioned that she'd heard great things about the service and that she'd use it herself if she could afford the fee." Suddenly, she rose from her chair. "I hate this. You're asking me to suspect people I trust. No, people I *trusted*."

Nick moved to her then and took her hands. "No, you don't have to suspect them. Just be willing to look at them objectively. Don't let your feelings blind you. And remember, we're theorizing here. *If* someone at Sheridan Trust is working with your bridegroom, they're very clever and so far they've covered their tracks pretty well. Before we leave, I want you to make a list of the people you work closely with and a list of the board members so that Sam can start checking them out." Then he turned to Sam. "Have you got anything in that stack of stuff that will shed some light on any of this?"

"I haven't been able to sort through all of it yet. There're some pictures, though." He sorted the pile into neat stacks and finally handed a sheet to Tyler. "It's a shot of a young man, the son of someone who worked for the Lawrences. He's about eighteen there, and the resolution's not so hot. But some of the old-timers who work for the Lawrence family say this is your Richard. He hung around the track a lot with the real Richard

Lawrence. His name is Jack Turnbull. They remember him as being a good mimic and having a way with horses, which is how he came to be friends with the real Lawrence. Jack liked to bet on the races even back then. Young Lawrence bailed him out once when he couldn't cover his bets. And he disappeared about the time the real Richard died."

"So he assumed the real Richard's identity, just like that?" Tyler asked.

Sam leaned back in his chair. "I'm only speculating, of course. But Richard was probably accepted at several colleges. Jack chose Columbia, a large campus a good distance away from where anyone might recognize him. It probably wasn't as difficult as you might imagine. And he evidently had a talent for winning people's confidence."

"Yes." Tyler nodded her head slowly as she stared at the picture of the boy and remembered the man she had thought she would marry. He looked very young in the picture but there was no mistaking the fact that he was Richard. No, she reminded herself. He was Jack. Briefly, she looked at the other people in the photo. Next to Jack was another young man grinning from ear to ear, and behind them were three older men, and a woman wearing a huge picture hat that hid most of her face. Something stirred then. A memory? Very carefully she let her gaze run over everyone in the photo again. Something pushed at the edge of her mind, then slipped away.

"What is it?" Nick asked.

Tyler shook her head. "Something seems almost familiar. It's probably the hat on the woman. They wear them all the time at the Kentucky Derby."

Turning back to Sam, Nick asked, "What else have you got here?"

"Files that go back two years on the clients using Personal Connections." He pushed a pile of papers toward them. "Now that we've got a real name on Jack Turnbull, we can trace his family and see where that leads."

"What we need is a connection between him and someone at Sheridan Trust." Nick turned to Tyler. "You can get started on that list now. Include everyone, even the board members, so that Sam can start checking them out. What we're looking for is anything that ties any of these people to Richard Lawrence or Jack Turnbull or to the Internet matchmaking service."

After handing Tyler a paper and pencil, Sam grinned and leaned back in his chair. "Damn, you're good. If you change your mind about California, I know they'd offer you a job here."

"This is just a little too organized for my taste," Nick said. "I was also hoping that you might get a line on these two goons who've been trying to snatch Tyler. One of them is called Louie."

By the time Nick described the two men to Sam, Tyler had completed her list. She was placing it on his desk when her cell phone rang.

All three of them stared at it as it rang a second time. Finally, Nick picked it up and handed it to Tyler. "Answer it."

Tyler put it to her ear. "Hello."

"Ms. Sheridan, is everything all right?"

Naomi's voice sounded strained in her ear. "Everything's fine. What's up?"

"Several board members have called. They each received anonymous notes this morning, saying that you are going to cancel the wedding."

Tyler met Nick's eyes. "Notes that I'm canceling the

wedding? And what have you been telling them, Naomi?"

"I've told them that it's a practical joke. And that if the wedding is to be canceled, you'll tell each one of them personally."

"Good," Tyler said. "You're handling it just right. Keep up the good work."

"Is there anything else I can do, Ms. Sheridan?"

Keeping her eyes steady on Nick's, she said, "Yes. Yes, there is. Do you by any chance remember how you first heard about Personal Connections?"

"Yes. It was your mother who told me about it."

"My mother? You're sure?"

"Absolutely. I'm not sure in what context it came up. It'll come to me, I'm sure. But she was quite enthusiastic. That much I do remember. That's why I've been wanting to give them a try."

"Thanks, Naomi. Continue to hold down the fort."

Tyler replaced the phone on the desk. "The board members are getting anonymous notes telling them that I'm canceling the wedding. And my mother is the person who told Naomi about Personal Connections. This must be my lucky day."

Nick moved to her and took her hands. "Naomi *claims* your mother told her. Remember, nothing's certain until all the letters fit into the squares."

As she looked into his eyes, the knots that had tightened in her stomach while she'd talked to Naomi loosened a bit. "You're right. But I still feel like Chicken Little."

"That's exactly how the kidnappers want you to feel. They want you desperate so that you'll meet their demands quickly."

"I want to catch them," she said, lifting her chin.

"Okay, I've got a plan. It's almost noon. You stay with Sam while I run over to the Plaza and wait for them to deliver the instructions."

Tyler smiled at him. "It's probably because you have so little experience formulating them, but your plan is lousy. I'm going with you."

"No. It'll be safer for you here. And it will give you a chance to go through that client list from Personal Connections, and see if any of the names look familiar."

"I can take that stuff with me." Removing her hands from Nick's, she grabbed the stack of faxes and tucked them under her arm. "Somebody is evidently trying to take my company away from me. And that ransom note might require me to take immediate action. Besides, we're partners. You can't leave me behind."

"You're partners?" Sam asked.

When they both turned to look at him, Sam raised both hands. "Sorry. It's just that I worked for Nick for four years and he wouldn't hear of making me his partner."

"She's prettier than you are," Nick said as he grabbed Tyler's free hand and walked out of his cousin's office.

THE LOBBY OF THE Plaza Hotel was crowded and noisy. The moment Nick spotted his friend Harry near the reception desk, he cut a path directly toward the man.

"I was just about to call you. An envelope arrived for Ms. Sheridan just a few minutes ago. If you'll step this way..."

Once Harry had ushered them into his office, he handed the envelope to Tyler and continued, "They used a different delivery service this time, but the same MO. It was paid for in cash, and the return address and phone number are fakes—just like the last one."

Tyler opened the envelope and read the instructions quickly. "They want one million in cash in denominations that will fit into a briefcase. More instructions will follow."

"One million in a briefcase," Nick repeated thoughtfully. "They want it easily portable. Are you going to have trouble coming up with that amount immediately?"

Tyler shook her head. "All I need to do is make a phone call. It will be here in a few hours."

"Who would know that you could get your hands on that kind of money so quickly on a Saturday?"

She met his eyes steadily. "The only person who could be sure of that is someone who knows that my grandmother always kept at least that amount in the safe at Sheridan Trust. She didn't ever want to be hampered just because it was a weekend. That would include Naomi, Howard, Richard, and perhaps even my mother—and who knows how many board members. I'll have to call Naomi, and she'll arrange to get it here."

Nick took her hands. "The squares aren't all filled in by a long shot."

"You can use my phone," Harry said.

FIFTEEN MINUTES LATER, Tyler sat at a table in the Palm Court. After setting down a pile of papers, she studied the man across from her. She hadn't missed Nick's hesitation when she'd said she didn't want to wait in her suite. But he hadn't argued, hadn't pointed out to her that Louie and his buddy knew that she hadn't checked out of the Plaza. Instead, he seemed to understand that she didn't want to go into hiding. That she couldn't let herself do that. It didn't even surprise her anymore that he was sensitive to other people's feelings.

"How do you stand the waiting?" she asked.

He glanced up from the menu. "By putting it to good use. This is going to be a working lunch. You're going to go through that stuff you took from Sam's office, and I'm going to check in with him and get updates as they occur."

"You didn't try to talk me out of paying the ransom."

"It wouldn't have done any good. I don't like to spend too much of my time banging my head against brick walls. That way I have energy for the battles I really want to win."

For a moment Tyler said nothing. He was talking about more than the kidnapping. Or was she just hoping he was?

Then slowly, Nick smiled.

"What's funny?" Tyler asked.

"I'm just enjoying seeing you sitting in the Palm Court dressed like that. Just yesterday, you fit in so perfectly. Now the fit isn't so good."

"Tyler? Is that you?"

"Howard?" At the sound of the voice, she whipped around, then rose from her seat as she recognized the distinguished, gray-haired man weaving his way through the tables toward her.

"What in the world is going on? You refuse to meet your mother and me for lunch. And then you show up with..." Howard turned to glare at Nick. "Who are you?"

"Howard—" Tyler placed a hand on his arm. She couldn't recall ever seeing him so upset. He looked as if he wanted to punch someone. "We're in a public place."

"Nick Romano from *Business Weekly*." Smiling, Nick slipped a card out of his wallet and handed it to the older man. "We're doing a feature article on up and coming CEOs, featuring Ms. Sheridan."

Howard frowned down at the card, then at Tyler. "I don't recall your mentioning this."

Tyler smiled. "With all the last-minute things to do for the wedding, it must have slipped my mind."

Howard looked her up and down, his frown deepening. "What are you doing in those clothes?"

"She's going to try some in-line skating," Nick said. "My photographers are meeting us this afternoon in Central Park. We want our readers to see what our country's CEOs do to relax."

"Skating?" Howard looked stunned. "How can you be thinking of something like that? Do you know—"

"Tyler? Is that you?"

This time when she recognized the voice and turned, her stomach plummeted right down to her toes. Hamilton Bradshaw and a slender girl of about twelve were just vacating a nearby table. Tyler had to work on the smile. "Mr. Bradshaw, this is such an unexpected pleasure."

"I'm taking my daughter to the ballet, a matinee performance, and we came here for a bite to eat first. I didn't expect to see you until tomorrow." He turned to Howard. "Howard." The older man shook Howard's hand enthusiastically, then introduced his daughter Cassie to each of them in turn until he reached Nick.

"I don't believe we've met before, Mr...."

"Nick Romano. I'm with *Business Weekly*." Nick shook Bradshaw's hand first, then Cassie's. "We're doing a feature on Ms. Sheridan. Rumor has it you're going to be doing business together."

Bradshaw waved a hand. "No comment on that.

We're still in negotiations." Turning to Tyler, he said, "Where's Richard?"

She'd known the question was coming, but she hadn't known what she was going to say until the answer popped out. "He's gone to visit his family in Kentucky. They've been estranged for years." Though she kept her eyes on Bradshaw, she heard Howard's quick intake of breath.

"Richard went to Kentucky?" Howard asked.

Tyler turned to him. "That's where his family is from. He wanted to mend some fences, invite them to the wedding. I encouraged him to go."

Bradshaw took her hand and patted it. "Good girl. In the end, family's the most important thing. Will he be back in time for our dinner tomorrow?"

"I hope so," Tyler said.

"Good. I'm looking forward to it." Bradshaw nodded at her, then smiled at Nick and Howard. "I have to get my daughter to the ballet. It's been a pleasure."

The moment he was out of earshot, Howard turned to Tyler, his gaze intense. "Why didn't you tell me Richard went to Kentucky?"

"He didn't want anyone to know. I told him I'd cover for him. Why are you so upset, Howard?"

"Is there a number he can be reached at?"

Tyler shook her head. "He didn't give me one. But he checks in every so often. Is there something you want me to tell him?"

Gripping her arm, Howard shot an impatient glance at Nick, then back at her. "We have to talk privately."

"No." Straightening her shoulders, Tyler drew herself up to her full height. "I've set aside the entire day for Mr. Romano."

Howard frowned at her. "There's an urgent matter

we have to discuss. I've been getting phone calls—" he lowered his voice "—from board members."

"Naomi has filled me in on that. She's handling it. Now, if you'll excuse me..." Moving quickly, she circled the next table and headed for the nearest exit. She was aware that Nick was following, but she didn't slacken her pace until Harry Putnam stepped into her path.

"Problem?" he asked.

By the time she drew in a breath, Nick had her arm and was saying, "Could you see that a lunch and any messages are delivered very discreetly to Ms. Sheridan's suite. And detain that gentleman who is following us until we can get there."

"It will be my pleasure," Harry said as he signaled two of his men to detain Howard Tremaine. "If you'll follow me, I'll show you where the private elevator to your suite is."

"He knows something," Tyler murmured as soon as she was sure they were far enough away from Howard. "He was frightened when I mentioned Kentucky."

"He's frightened about something," Nick agreed. "Maybe Sam will have some news soon."

A few minutes later, they were in the elevator shooting upward. Nick tightened his grip on the railing that ran along the mirrored back wall, while emotions warred inside him. She'd stood up to Tremaine and handled Bradshaw like a pro. But her bravado had faded the moment the elevator doors had slid shut. He wanted to reach out to her, touch her. But the last thing she needed right now was another person questioning her and making demands. Patience had never been his long suit, but he searched for it now.

He couldn't let either one of them think about the future right now. Not as long as the very real danger she was in existed in the present. And if he was going to help her, he had to hang onto his objectivity and concentrate on the now. That was the rule that had defined his success as a PI.

Never had he had so much trouble biding by it.

The moment the doors slid open, she reached for his hand and linked her fingers with his. The pain that had banded tightly around his heart eased a little. The door to the suite was directly in front of him.

"What do you do when everything seems to be blowing up in your face?" she asked.

"Easy," he said. "I deal with it one step at a time. Wait here." Taking her hand, he pressed her fingers against the button that would keep the doors open. Then he drew his gun. "I'm going to check out the rooms. If anything happens, press the button for the lobby. Harry will take it from there."

At her nod, he moved forward, inserted a card into the lock and, when the green light blinked, flattened himself against the wall and pushed open the door. Going in low, he flipped on the light switch and swept the room with his gaze and his gun. It was a huge suite with a sunken sitting area and a kitchen blocked off at one end. Empty. Moving forward quickly, he checked behind counters and drapes before he moved on to search two bedrooms and two adjoining baths. When he returned quickly to the small foyer, Tyler was still standing in the elevator where he'd left her.

"It's safe," he said.

She moved past him into the room. The moment he'd locked the door behind them, she said, "For the first time in my life I don't want to think of the future."

"That's understandable. You'll feel better once you eat something."

She shook her head. "I don't even want to be Tyler Sheridan anymore."

He turned to study her. "What do you want?"

"You."

It was a word he'd have begged to hear in other circumstances. "Tyler, I..."

She moved to him then. "Please. Can't we pretend? I want to go back to that moment when I first walked into your office. Only, you're not Nick Romano, the man my grandmother sent me to. You're just a man, and I'm just a woman. Can we just pretend for a little while?"

Whatever battle he was waging within himself was lost. If that was what she needed right now, he couldn't deny her. He might not be able to make sure that she didn't lose her company, but he could give her this. Smiling slowly, he said, "Okay, we're strangers, and we've never met before."

She drew in a breath and said, "Do you know what I wanted to do more than anything when I first saw you sleeping on that couch?"

"What?"

"This—" She ran one hand lightly up his chest, then the other. "I'd never experienced anything like it before. I felt as if I would die if I didn't touch you. I felt I might die if I did. Then you leaped up, so dangerous looking. I wanted to touch you even more."

Her words had his mind clouding, his blood thickening. He wanted to reach for her, but he wasn't sure he could lift his arms.

"And then I would have done this." Rising on her toes, she brushed her lips against his, then withdrew, moving her mouth to his ear. "Once I started, I wouldn't have been able to stop myself."

Her words were only a whispered breath in his ear. They shot straight to his center, fueling a fire that was already burning.

Her teeth nipped his earlobe. "Let me tell you what I wanted you to do to me."

And she did.

The urgent, husky whisper sent explosions rippling through him even before she wrapped her arms around him and pressed her mouth against his. His mind went blank. And then as he dragged her close, it began to fill with her, with the fantasy that her words had created. When the richness of her flavor poured through him, he should have been prepared for it. But it seemed new, different. As if it were the first time he'd kissed her. Pushing her cap off, he ran his fingers through her hair and then fisted his hands in it and dove even more deeply into the kiss. He had to have it all.

Heat radiated from her, burning into him until he was sure he'd been caught in a furnace. With a sudden oath, he ripped the shirt from her. Buttons pinged against the wall as he dragged her to the floor. Then he began to feast on her, taking his hands on a quick, rough journey over soft skin and taut, smooth muscles.

She was driving him mad, her scent tempting him. It was so subtle beneath her breast—he wanted to linger there, but he couldn't. Because it was stronger, more tempting where her skin curved in at her waist. Impatient, he tore at the snap of her jeans and dragged them down her legs. And then he had to taste and taste. He wanted to savor the sweetness at her hipbone but he had to move lower. How could he resist when she trembled and her legs parted for him?

Her mind was filled with him, and with each new pleasure he was bringing her. So many sensations were battering through her. Each time she thought there couldn't be anything more, there suddenly was. His hands had touched her everywhere, her body was burning, and now his mouth was hovering over her very core. She gasped for a breath. If she could just get one, she could tell him—to stop, to go on. But her voice seemed trapped in her throat, just as her body was trapped in the pleasure he brought her, the pleasure that was yet to come. For a second, an eternity, time seemed to stand still. Each separate sensation shot through her: the press of his fingers into her hips, the whisper of his breath moving into her, and then, finally, the touch of his tongue. It freed the sound that was trapped in her throat. *Nick.*

Desperate for him, she arched upward as the heat poured into her. Her heart had surely never beaten this fast. Her body had never yearned so much. And an ache, huge and consuming, began to swell in her. She reached out to him then, fisting her hands in his hair, calling out his name, as the first climax shook her. There was only him.

For seconds, she floated free and weightless, before she began to spiral down. And then he sent the second climax shuddering through her.

When she could breathe, when she could find the strength to tighten her grip on him, she drew him upward. "I want you inside me. Now."

Her face was all he could see as he rose above her. Her hair was spread on the carpet, her eyes were the color of the sea at night. "Tell me you're mine," he demanded as he slipped just barely inside her.

"I'm yours," she whispered, arching upward.

Only then did he drive himself in. As her softness enclosed him, all he knew was her. Together they began to move, racing harder, faster, to a place they'd never been before. It was dark. He could see nothing but her. Only her. The air burned in his lungs, blocking the sound as he cried out her name.

Weakened and spent, he had no idea how long he lay on top of her before his brain began to function again. She was still trembling. So was he. He couldn't think clearly enough to sort what she'd made him feel into separate sensations. All he knew was that she felt as soft as water beneath him, and he could have floated this way forever.

It was a struggle, but eventually he summoned up the strength to lever himself up and rest his weight on his forearms. Her eyes were open and on his. He felt as if he were drowning all over again. "Only you," he whispered as he brushed his lips over hers.

His kiss was gentle and undemanding, but the moment she responded and stirred beneath him, he began to harden again. *Impossible,* he thought, as he moved his mouth over hers again. But it wasn't, he discovered, as passion took control again.

10

HE COULDN'T take his eyes off her. He didn't want to. She was sitting on the sunken floor of the living room, squinting her way through the stack of faxes and papers she'd taken from Sam's office. She was wearing his flannel shirt. The remains of the lunch they'd shared still lay on the floor surrounding her. In a moment, he'd clear it away, but for now he could give in to the urge simply to watch her.

He could admire her efficiency. The method she'd developed of running her finger quickly down a page, then discarding it into a neat pile would allow her to sort through everything in record time.

He admired her energy, too. She hadn't slept after they'd made love, though he'd urged her to. If was as if her brief escape from the burden of being Tyler Sheridan had given her the strength she needed to assume the role again. When he'd jokingly accused her of merely using him, she'd laughed, kissed him soundly, and promised to do it again.

He was going to hold her to that. And more. But first, they had a problem to solve. Somewhere in that pile of papers she was plowing through was a name that would reshuffle the facts they'd already gathered and slip everything into its proper square.

And then they would have a different kind of problem to solve.

She looked up and met his eyes. "You're staring at me."

"Yep. I'm discovering new things about you."

"Such as?"

"You need glasses."

"How do you know that?"

"I have the fine-honed observational skills of a top-notch private eye."

Tyler leaned back against one of the love seats and pinched the bridge of her nose. "Right. How could I have forgotten that?"

"What have you got so far?"

She sighed and turned to put the sheet she'd been scrutinizing in a discard pile, then picked up another. "A lot of people used Personal Connections in the past five years. So far, I've only seen two names that I recognize: Richard's and mine."

"How many more names do you have to look through?"

"It's an alphabetical list. I'm just finishing the Ss. You must have hated this part of PI work," she said as she ran her finger down the list of names on the next sheet.

"Why do you say that?"

She shot him a quick look before she turned her attention back to the list. "Patience is a quality that doesn't come easily to you."

"I work at it," he said. And he couldn't recall that it had ever been quite this hard before.

"Good grief," she said suddenly.

"What?"

"My mother." She met his eyes then. "Before she married Howard, she was Claudia Stafford. That name is on this list."

"Is there a sheet that shows if she matched up with someone?"

Tyler shuffled through papers. "No...wait." She met Nick's eyes again. "Howard's name is here, too. He never told me he used it. And if he met my mother through Personal Connections, he never said a word about it."

"Did they both know that you used Personal Connections to meet Richard?"

"Howard did. He knew that I was getting Richard's background checked out. He might have told my mother. I didn't. We don't talk much."

"It's interesting that he didn't mention using the service," Nick said, stepping down into the sunken living room. "What else have you got there?"

"Just the pictures that Sam got from his operative in Kentucky."

He spread them out in front of her, then settled himself at her side. "Look at them again. There was something in one of them that tugged at your memory. See if you can jar it loose."

As she picked the first one up and squinted down at it, he fished his keys out of his pocket and handed them to her. "Try the magnifying glass on the key ring."

She did, studying each picture in turn. It was while she was looking at the last one that she began to frown. He knew exactly when she recognized something by the way she stiffened. "I'm almost sure it's my mother in this picture. I can't see her face. It's the hat I remember. She had one just like this when I was thirteen. She was between husbands, and we spent a month together. I remember trying on the hat."

"That would have been twelve years ago. The timing is right. Are you sure about the hat?"

Tyler set the paper down on her lap for a minute and rubbed her hands together.

"What is it?" Nick asked.

"My fingers are tingling. But I can't be sure."

"A lot of people could have had the same hat," Nick said.

"It isn't just the hat," Tyler said, picking up the magnifying glass and handing it to him. "I recognize the dress, too. And one of the men in the back row. You take a look and tell me."

Nick felt his thumbs start to prick the moment he glanced down at the picture. The power of suggestion, he thought as he carefully studied the first man standing behind Jack Turnbull. The resolution was grainy, but from what he could see, the guy had a narrow face, jutting cheekbones and a high forehead with thinning hair. He'd never seen him before. It was the man standing next to him that had his eyes narrowing. Frowning, he studied it for a few minutes. The man had dark hair and wore a mustache. In the picture he was smiling. Earlier when Nick had seen him in the Palm Court, the man hadn't been wearing the mustache, his hair was graying, and he hadn't been happy. Mentally, Nick made the adjustments. Finally, he said, "It could be Howard Tremaine."

"I'm almost sure it is." Tyler folded her hands tightly in her lap. "If Howard and my mother knew each other twelve years ago, and they knew Jack Turnbull and the real Richard Lawrence, too... Even though I'm not a licensed PI, I can come up with a theory that puts a lot of what we know into neat little squares."

"Yeah," Nick said, covering her clasped hands with his. "But I still have a lot of questions. If they already knew each other, why go to Personal Connections?"

"I've got a bigger one," Tyler said, pressing her fingers against her temples. "Why would she and Howard join forces with Richard—I mean Jack Turnbull—to betray me?"

"Maybe they want to run Sheridan Trust."

"But they'd have a better chance of doing that with me as CEO. The board isn't going to appoint either of them."

"Good point," Nick said, tilting up her chin and giving her a quick kiss. "Did I ever tell you I admire the way your mind works?"

"My mind feels like it's caught in a whirlpool right now."

Nick smiled at her. "That's a good sign. Let everything swirl around. When it settles, we may be able to see an entirely different pattern."

When the phone rang, Tyler immediately tensed.

"It's got to be either Sam or Harry. No other calls are to be put through." Nick reached for the extension on a nearby table. "Yeah... Bring it up... Okay, I'll tell her." Placing his hand over the mouthpiece, he turned to Tyler. "The money just arrived, and Harry says your mother is desperate to talk to you."

Tyler sighed. "Howard probably told her about the letters the board members have received, and she's worried about the wedding arrangements."

"She might have some answers if you're up to talking to her."

She rubbed her hands absently together and then on her jeans. "You're right. I'd like to hear what she has to say about this picture. Not on the phone, though," she added. "I want to show it to her and see her face."

Nick took his hand off the phone. "I'll have Harry bring the money up when he escorts your mother."

TYLER ROSE when she heard the knock on the door. It didn't surprise her that her fingers had begun to prick again. They always did when she was with her mother. They'd been close once, but they'd chosen such different paths in life.

When Nick opened the door, he stood completely still for a count of three before he stepped out of the way so that Claudia Sheridan Coleman Stafford Tremaine could enter the suite. Though Tyler was aware that Nick was taking a briefcase from Harry, she kept her eyes on her mother. She'd been told that she resembled Claudia, but Tyler had never seen it. No one ever reacted to her the way they did when her mother walked into a room. Claudia's looks were more dramatic in every way. There were fiery highlights in her blond hair and her eyes were a deeper shade of blue. Today, her bronzed skin offered a stunning contrast to the white linen sundress she was wearing. And though she was clearly agitated, she'd taken the time to give Nick a thorough look before she'd stepped down into the sunken living room and crossed to Tyler.

"Howard told me that he's getting phone calls from board members. Is it true? Have you canceled the wedding?"

Tyler had given some thought to what she would say, and this time she decided to go with the truth. "Richard's been kidnapped."

Claudia's mouth opened, then shut as she sank down on a nearby love seat. "That's... Tell me you're joking."

"I wish I were. You can't tell anyone, not even Howard," Tyler said. "If it were to leak to the press, Richard's life might be in danger."

Claudia's eyes grew wide with shock. Her hand fluttered to her chest as if she were having trouble getting a breath. "Who? Do you have any idea?"

Tyler shook her head, struggling to shove her emotions down. Handle it like a board meeting. That was the plan she'd developed while she'd waited for her mother's arrival.

"Could I offer you a drink, Mrs. Tremaine?" Nick asked.

Claudia glanced up at him. "Yes. Vodka with a twist." Then her eyes narrowed. "Who are you? What are you doing here in my daughter's suite?"

Nick extended his hand. "Nick Romano. I'm with the FBI's Manhattan Bureau, and I've been assigned to the case."

Claudia shook his hand, then turned back to Tyler. "Are they asking for a ransom?"

"Yes. For one million in cash, they'll return him tomorrow, unharmed, and the wedding can take place on schedule. I think the letters to the board members were just to pressure me into paying the money quickly."

"Don't pay it."

Tyler blinked at the firmness in her mother's tone.

Claudia rose to take her daughter's hands. "I'm sorry. I shouldn't have said that. In your place...I'm not sure what I would do. And Howard—" she paused to shake her head "—Howard and your grandmother would want me to remind you that you have to do what's best for Sheridan Trust. It's just that this is your wedding day, the most wonderful day of your life, and someone is spoiling it...for money. I don't think they should get away with it."

Tyler squeezed her mother's hands and decided to go with the truth again. "Mother, I need your help."

"What can I do?"

"You have to promise not to tell anyone."

"I won't if you don't want me to."

"We have to have your word on that, Mrs. Tremaine," Nick interjected.

Claudia looked from Tyler to Nick and then back again. "You have my word."

Releasing her mother's hands, Tyler picked up the fax of the newspaper photo. "Is this you in the picture?"

Claudia studied it for a minute, frowning. "Where did you get this?"

"It doesn't matter. I recognized the hat. You let me try it on once. Did you know Howard twelve years ago?"

Claudia nodded, not taking her eyes off the picture. "That was when I was first married to Ralph Stafford. He raised horses in California, and I met Howard when we went to Kentucky for some of the races. He was an accountant and investment manager for some of the people Ralph knew. We ran into him at parties and at the track."

"Do you recognize Richard Lawrence?" Tyler asked.

Claudia studied the picture again. "Ralph stabled the horses he was racing at the Lawrences' farm. I think he's the man standing next to Howard."

"I'm talking about *my* Richard, his son."

Claudia frowned. "I don't know...unless he's one of the young men in the foreground?"

"Who is Jack Turnbull?" Tyler asked.

Claudia looked at her. "I have no idea who he is. This picture was taken so many years ago. What does it have to do with Richard's disappearance?"

"Are you sure you don't recognize either of those young men?"

Claudia glanced back down at the picture for a minute. Finally, she shook her head. "They're just kids. Ralph and I had only been married for a few months, and I wasn't thinking about much of anything or anyone but him." She frowned thoughtfully. "I can't even remember when this picture was taken. It must have been at the racetrack where one of Ralph's horses was running. I wasn't even posing. You can't see my face because I was too busy looking at Ralph."

Lies or the truth? From his vantage point behind the kitchen counter, Nick wasn't sure he could tell. But if she was lying, Claudia Tremaine was one hell of an actress. Just as her daughter was turning out to be one hell of an interrogator. As he filled a glass with ice and vodka, he watched Tyler pinch the bridge of her nose briefly. She had a headache. He turned a flame on under a teakettle before he carried Claudia's drink into the living room.

"If you knew Howard back then, weren't you surprised when you met him again through Personal Connections?" Tyler asked.

Claudia dropped the paper and stared at Tyler. "How did you know?"

"I have a copy of the client list that goes back two years. That's just about when you met, isn't it?"

Claudia sank slowly into the love seat again. When Nick handed her the vodka, she took a quick sip, then held the glass tightly in both hands. "We thought it was fate."

"Did Howard tell you that's where I met Richard?"

"Yes, he did." Raising her eyes, she met Tyler's. "I asked him not to tell you that we'd used Personal Connections. I thought if he did, you wouldn't use them simply because I had. I had such good luck meeting Howard through them. I wanted you to meet someone, too." Drawing in a deep breath and letting it out, she continued, "I know that you don't approve of the way I've lived my life, the choices I've made. You've never forgiven me for marrying again so soon after your father died."

"Mother, you don't have to—"

"No, I'd like to say this. The one thing that I regret was going along with your decision to stay with your grandmother. I thought it would only be temporary, that you'd forgive me. But it drove a wedge between us. I could see that you were never going to look twice at any of the young men I introduced you to. So I recommended Personal Connections to Naomi in the hope that she'd suggest it to you."

"What about later? After Richard and I were engaged? Why didn't you mention it then?"

After taking another sip of her drink, Claudia set it down on a table, then met her daughter's eyes again. "I didn't see the point. I was just glad you had someone in your life. I haven't been much of a mother to you, but I didn't want you to end up alone like your grandmother."

The moment he heard the hiss of steam, Nick retreated to the kitchen area and brewed a cup of tea. He didn't envy Tyler the job she was doing. It couldn't be easy grilling her mother. He'd be going through hell if he had to question Gina. But Tyler was handling the job like a pro. Each time she reached an impasse with Claudia, she would take a new tack. Locating a package of pain relievers in a first aid kit, he placed it on a tray with the mug of tea and then waited for a break in the conversation.

"Did Howard ever mention why he decided to use

Personal Connections? He doesn't seem to me the kind of man who would have trouble getting a date."

"He wasn't looking for a 'date,'" Claudia said. "He wanted marriage. He'd been one of the original investors in the company, and so he decided since it was so successful, he might as well give it a try."

"And how did you first hear of it?" Tyler asked.

Claudia shook her head. "I don't recall exactly. I might have heard about it where I play tennis. Or it might have been during the week I spent at a spa out in California." She shrugged and waved a hand. "It will come to me when I'm not trying so hard to remember. In the meantime—" she picked up the picture again "—who is this Jack Turnbull you were asking about?"

"We think he might be behind Richard's kidnapping," Nick said as he set the tea tray down in front of Tyler and handed her the painkillers.

"Howard probably knows who he is," Claudia said. "I could ask him."

"We don't want you to do that," Nick said. "We don't even want him to know that Richard's been kidnapped."

"All right." Claudia shifted her gaze from Nick to Tyler. "I won't breathe a word. What else can I do to help?"

"Nothing right now," Tyler said, rising. "Except perhaps to keep Howard from worrying too much. He was nearly frantic in the lobby a while ago."

"Keeping Howard calm is one thing that I can do very well. But I wish I could do more." She stood up and took Tyler's hands in hers. "I've always meant the best. I love you."

"I love you, too, Mom," she said as she walked her mother to the door. The moment she shut it, she turned and leaned against it. "I believe her. Is it just because I want to?"

Nick moved to her then and, putting his arms around her, just held her. "I think I believe her, too."

Tyler sighed and rested her head against him for a moment. "That leaves Howard."

"Yeah," Nick said. "An original investor in Personal Connections might have access to the questionnaires. But before we tackle him, I want you to take those pills, drink that tea and lie down for a power nap."

"Power nap?"

"It's some CEO talk I picked up. How about if I throw in a back rub?" he asked as he led her back to the sofa.

"Back rub. Let me guess. That must be FBI talk."

Nick was laughing as he began to knead the muscles at the back of her neck.

THE RINGING OF THE PHONE had Tyler scrambling up and off the couch. It took her just a second to orient herself. She was standing in the sunken living room of the suite in the Plaza. A quick glance at her watch told her she hadn't been asleep long. Twenty minutes tops. She could recall glancing at her watch just as Nick had started to massage her temples where her headache had been pounding. The second ring made her frown. It wasn't the hotel phone, so it had to be her cell phone. Where was Nick? Hurrying into the bedroom, she recognized the sound of the shower running and located her phone on the dresser. "Hello?"

"Ms. Sheridan, it's Naomi. I've just spoken with Richard, and he said it was urgent that I pass this message along to you."

"What did he say?"

"It didn't make much sense to me. But he said you'd

understand, that you'd better. It was just three sentences. He told me to write them down exactly. Remember Mama. Remember where we shared our first kiss. Remember to bring the briefcase and come alone."

"That's it?"

"I asked him that same question. That's when he made me write it down. Then he told me that he'd see me next Saturday at the wedding."

"Thank you, Naomi. If he calls back with any other messages and I'm not here, you can give them to Nick Romano. Can you remember that name?"

"I've got it written down."

For a few moments after she hung up, Tyler stared straight ahead. The three sentences were swirling around in her mind while a tight ball of fear settled in her stomach. *Remember Mama*—it couldn't mean what she thought it did. Hurrying into the living room, she picked up the room phone and spoke to the operator. "Please connect me to Mrs. Howard Tremaine's room."

She paced back and forth while she counted the rings. On the sixth one, it was Howard's voice she finally heard. "Howard, this is Tyler. I want to speak to my mother."

"I thought she was with you. That hotel dick escorted her up to your suite over an hour ago, and I haven't seen her since."

"She left here about forty-five minutes ago, and she said she was headed for your room."

"She hasn't gotten here yet. Tyler, what in the world is going on? We have to talk. Let me come up there."

"Later," Tyler said as she hung up. *Remember Mama.* The fear was streaming through her. Those two words could only mean one thing. Jack must have Claudia. And she knew what the rest of the message meant, too.

She knew exactly where she had to take the money and that she had to come alone. Glancing toward the bedroom door, she grabbed the hotel notepaper and pen. The sound of the shower had stopped, and she didn't have much time to leave Nick a note.

NICK STEPPED OUT of the bedroom and glanced over to where he'd left Tyler dozing on the couch. When he didn't see her, he walked to the other bedroom door and opened it. Empty. He felt the first prickle of unease as he moved to search the bathroom. "Tyler?" By the time he made it back into the living room of the suite, he was pushing back the fear that was threatening to wash over him. It broke free the moment he saw that the briefcase containing the money was gone.

And then he saw the note next to the phone.

Nick— I got a call from Naomi. Jack has my
mother. I'm taking the money to a place along the
bridle path in Central Park. He said to come alone.
I've drawn you a map.

Cramming the note in his pocket, he raced for the door. Nick cursed under his breath all the way down to the lobby. It kept him from thinking about what could happen to Tyler once Jack got hold of her. She couldn't have more than a ten-minute head start on him. That meant he had time. It *had* to mean that he still had time.

The moment the elevator doors slid open, he hurried toward the main entrance that opened out onto the park. Before he could reach it, Howard Tremaine stepped into his path.

"You're not with *Business Weekly*. I checked. I want to know who you are."

Nick gripped Howard's lapels, nearly lifting him off the floor. "Who's Jack Turnbull?"

Howard blanched, and the hands he'd fisted went slack. "How do you know about Jack?"

"I know he's got your wife, and Tyler is going to meet him right now. You better pray that he doesn't hurt either one of them. And if you're involved, so help me—"

"You're crazy." Howard licked his lips. "Jack wouldn't hurt them."

"Problem?" Harry asked as he stepped to Nick's side.

Ignoring Harry, Nick spoke softly to Howard, "Someone who's spent the past twelve years masquerading as someone else doesn't have a lot of credibility with me. Especially when he's made three attempts to kidnap Tyler already."

"Kidnap?" Pausing, Howard licked his lips again. "He's got Claudia?"

"That's what he told Tyler." Releasing Howard, Nick turned to Harry and fished out the map that Tyler had drawn. "I need to get to this spot in the park—she says it's a bridge about a quarter mile from where the old stables used to be."

"C'mon," Harry said. "I'll get you a taxi driver who knows the park."

"I'm coming with you," Howard said, as they strode toward the revolving doors. Before Nick could object, he said, "I might know where they are. I used to go riding there with Jack."

"And why should I trust you?" Nick asked.

"Because Jack's my stepson. I may be able to talk some sense into him."

OVERHEAD, the pewter colored clouds were thick with the threat of rain. Tyler felt the hair sticking to the back of her neck as she walked quickly along the path. The air was still and breathless.

With every step she took, the words *Remember Mama* beat in her head. Because she didn't want to think of the very real danger her mother could be in, she made herself think instead of the first time she'd ridden here with the man she'd believed to be Richard Lawrence. The weather had been cooler, sunny, a perfect day for a ride. It had been their second date. Their first one had been a no-pressure drink in the Oak Room of the Plaza. He'd suggested it, and they'd talked for two hours. It had seemed a wonderful coincidence when they discovered they shared a love of horses.

But it hadn't been a coincidence at all. He'd known that she loved horses because he'd known everything about her. Nick had been right all along. Somehow Jack must have gotten access to her questionnaire. Tyler could feel the anger bubbling up in her as she thought of how she'd been manipulated. She welcomed the feeling. It would help her keep the fear under control.

Without breaking stride, she switched the briefcase to her other hand. On the taxi ride from the hotel, she'd tried to come up with a plan but had drawn a blank. The important thing was to make sure her mother was safe. After that, she'd have to play it by ear.

But one thing she knew—Jack Turnbull was not going to get away with this. When she heard a rider approaching, she moved to the side of the bridle path and waited for him to pass. The place that Richard...no, that *Jack* had chosen was far enough from the path that no one would see. She'd done her best to draw the location on the little map she'd left for Nick. But there hadn't been much time, and she'd had to rely on memory. The break in the trees ahead was just as she recalled, but would Nick be able to spot it?

Setting her briefcase down, she flipped it open and removed a package of fifties. Then she stuck one on a low branch of a tree. Hansel and Gretel had used bread crumbs. Nick would have to settle for cold hard cash.

Quickening her pace, Tyler left the path and started up an incline. The bridge should be to the left. But even now, she was relying on instinct as much as memory to guide her. She left fifties on bushes to mark her direction. In the distance, she could hear the faint sounds of traffic, but it was hard to imagine when she looked around that this place existed in the middle of Manhattan. That was what had struck her that first morning. Jack had brought her here for privacy, so that he could kiss her without being interrupted. But the isolation that had charmed her then frightened her now. If she screamed, if her mother screamed, no one would hear them. And she didn't know what Jack Turnbull might be capable of.

She paused the moment the bridge came into view. It was deserted. For a moment, she felt fear swell within her. Then she moved forward. Of course, he wouldn't be waiting out in plain sight. He was under the bridge.

And he was, sitting on a horse, her mother in front of him, and he had a gun pointed at her. He waited, not moving, as Tyler slipped and slid down the steep incline. Loosened stones crashed to the path below.

"That's far enough," he said when she was about fifteen feet away. "You brought the money?"

As she set the briefcase down, Tyler studied the man on the horse. He'd changed. The Richard she'd known had been charming and smooth. Reasonable. The tension in this man spoke of desperation. Even his tone of voice was different. He was Jack Turnbull, and she had to figure out a way to keep him here until Nick arrived. But first she had to get her mother off the horse.

"Open it," Jack said.

Tyler didn't move. "Mom, are you all right?"

"Yes," Claudia said.

"Help her down from the horse," Tyler said.

"Not before I see the money," Jack replied.

Overhead, thunder rumbled. The horse whinnied and began to prance.

"If he rears up," Jack said, "your mother might fall."

Tyler dropped to her knees, opened the briefcase, then angled it so that Jack could see the neatly packaged bundles of cash.

"Now hand it to me," Jack said.

"Let my mother down from the horse first."

Jack moved his mount forward. "You always did have a stubborn streak, Tyler. But your mother's going to stay with me for a while. Just in case you didn't follow my instructions to come alone. She's my insurance until I can get to where I'm going."

As he drew alongside her, Tyler could see only traces of the man she'd known and become engaged to. This man, Jack, would pull the trigger if he had to. Pushing down the fear, she said, "How about an exchange? You let my mother down, and I'll come with you, instead."

"Tyler, don't—" Her mother's sentence ended on a quick intake of breath when Jack shoved the barrel of the gun into her side.

"You let her go, and I'll come with you quietly," Tyler said.

Jack studied Tyler for a minute. "You've got a deal. Hand me the briefcase first."

Rising, she lifted up the briefcase, releasing it only

when Claudia had swung her leg over and was sliding toward the ground. Once her hand was free, Tyler pulled her mother close and breathed in her ear, "Get up to the top of the bridge." Then turning, she focused her attention on Jack. In the time it took him to fasten the briefcase to the saddle, she nudged Claudia behind her and backed away a few paces.

"Not so fast," Jack said, aiming the gun at her. "Swing up behind me."

Tyler stayed right where she was. She had to stall. Each second brought Nick closer. She had to believe that.

"Give me your hand," Jack said, extending his.

"I will just as soon as my mother is out of range of your gun."

"Tyler, I don't have time—"

Thunder rumbled again, this time closer, and the horse did a quick sidestep. Tyler took the opportunity to step forward, grabbing the bridle and patting the horse's neck. Behind her, she could track the sound of her mother's progress. When the horse had settled, she looked up at its rider.

"Why are you doing this, Jack?"

His eyes narrowed. "You know who I am? That PI you ran to must be good."

"He's a heck of a lot better than the security people at Sheridan Trust who checked out Richard Lawrence. Did Howard have anything to do with that?"

Jack gave a short laugh. "Are you kidding? Howard wouldn't help me. He wanted to tell you all about me, but I convinced him that I'd made a new life for myself as Richard Lawrence, I'd learned from my mistakes, and I hadn't gambled in years. And I hadn't—not under the name of Richard Lawrence, anyway. Your security people just weren't thorough enough. But then, why look for a death record if you believe the person is alive and kicking?"

She could see that some of the tension had eased out of him now that he had the money and she'd promised to go with him. If she could just keep him talking... "What about those two men in the black van? Did you send them after me?"

"I had to get you away from that PI. If you hadn't hired him, everything would be different. We'd still be getting married."

"How did you get access to my questionnaire at Personal Connections?"

"You figured that out, too?" When she didn't answer, he smiled. "I used to have a relationship with one of the women who created the company. She'd 'tinkered' with other questionnaires for a few very generous clients, but her partner caught on and wanted to buy her out. Before my friend took the deal, she told me I could browse through some records if I wanted to marry a millionaire. When I saw your name on one of the questionnaires, I knew it was a match made in heaven."

Thunder rumbled again. This time, Tyler kept a tight grip on the bridle. A few drops began to fall. Out of the corner of her eye, she was almost sure she'd seen some movement on the bridge overhead.

"Why? Out of all the women you could have chosen, why pick me?"

NICK CURSED STEADILY under his breath as he jogged along the bridle path. It was helping to keep his fear at bay. But nothing seemed to push from his mind the image of two defenseless women and a desperate man. Howard's claim that he'd known the bridge Tyler had scribbled on the map hadn't panned out, and precious minutes had been lost. Once they'd reached the spot where the old stables had been, Nick had insisted that they fan out, and he'd taken the route that seemed to fit the one Tyler had drawn.

A quarter of a mile, he thought to himself. It was hardly long enough to break a sweat, but perspiration was already dripping into his eyes. Stopping, he wiped it from his forehead, and scanned the path for a break in the trees. Spotting one up ahead, he started toward it as thunder rumbled in the distance. How was he supposed to be sure that this "break" was the one Tyler was referring to?

Then he saw the fifty-dollar bill pierced through its center by one of the branches, and he nearly laughed out loud. He would later, he promised himself. Once he found her, he and Tyler would laugh together.

"WHY YOU?" JACK ASKED. "There are literally a million reasons. For starters, you could take a look in the mirror. Not all millionaires are beautiful."

Once again, Tyler ignored the hand he extended, turning to murmur something to the horse.

"Tyler, I'm losing patience."

She raised her eyes to meet his, and over his shoulder she saw someone crouched behind the railing of the bridge. Nick? She had to keep Jack talking. "There's something I have to know. If you needed money that desperately, why did you try to orchestrate your own kidnapping? Why didn't you just ask me?"

"Howard would never have stood for my borrowing any money from you. And I had to have it fast. I've been having some bad luck at the track, and one of my creditors is on my case. I've only been able to stall him this long because of the wedding."

When the thunder sounded, she murmured to the horse and moved him closer to the shelter beneath the bridge. When he'd settled, she raised her eyes to Richard's again.

"Howard doesn't control me. He couldn't have stopped me."

Growing impatient, Richard fastened his fingers around her wrist and jerked her closer to him. "He didn't have to. He stopped me from asking. He would have pulled the plug on me the instant he suspected I might be gambling again."

Resisting his pull on her hand, Tyler stared at him for a minute. "Why didn't he tell me right in the beginning?"

"Because Howard's my stepfather, and he didn't want you or your mother to know about the favor he did for me in Kentucky. There were some very nasty people after me back then, and Howard offered to help wipe the slate clean for me. If my mother had still been alive, she would have asked him to. He made it clear that he was doing it for her. As the business manager for the Lawrences, he arranged for me to enter one of the colleges Richard was accepted to. He took care of all the paperwork."

As Jack continued to talk, Tyler patted the horse's neck, coaxing him to inch backward closer to the bridge. In her peripheral vision, she could see that it was Nick on the bridge and that he'd thrown one leg over the railing. He was going to jump down. If he tried to come down the incline on either side, Jack would have plenty of time to shoot him. If she could just get the horse closer...

Thunder rolled noisily across the sky, and Tyler saw lightning spark in the distance. This time when the horse tried to rear, she strengthened her grip on the bridle and backed it up two steps. She was almost close enough.

Jack pulled her arm. "C'mon, Tyler. Get on the horse."

"You don't have to run," Tyler said. "There's an alternative. You can keep the money and we could go through with our marriage next Saturday."

Those were the last words she said before Nick leaped off the bridge and plummeted downward on top of Jack. As the two men pitched to the ground, the rain began to come down in earnest. The horse reared and she grabbed the reins, keeping a tight hold as it reared again. By the time she turned to the two men, Nick was grabbing Jack by the seat of his pants to keep him from escaping up the incline. Then they were rolling downward, a jumble of limbs.

The struggle was brief but fierce. For Tyler, it became a series of images, alternately lit with lightning and blocked by sheets of rain. Jack on top of Nick, the gun still in his hand. Nick with a viselike grip on Jack's wrist, heaving him off. Both men struggling to their feet, coming together in a deadly, fierce embrace and crashing again to the ground.

The flash of fire as the gun went off.

During the endless moment when neither of the men moved, Tyler felt time stop.

Then slowly, the man on top rose. Tyler only fully registered that it was Nick when his arms were around her and she felt his heart beating against hers.

11

TYLER STARED OUT the window of her office at Sheridan Trust. Dusk was quickly slipping into night. Just as Nick was slowly, surely slipping out of her life. That was the fear she'd been living with for two days. Turning away from the darkening sky, she began to pace the floor of her office.

The last time she'd seen Nick had been at the precinct where they'd all been taken for questioning. During the maelstrom of explaining everything to the police, and then to her mother and Howard, she'd only caught glimpses of him. Later, she'd found he'd been busy making sure all the loose ends of the case against Jack Turnbull were tied up. Once Louie and his buddy had been arrested and charged, they'd been eager to make a deal. She'd also learned Nick had used every contact he had to see that only the barest details of the incident were leaked to the press. A man named Jack Turnbull and two accomplices had been arrested for attempted kidnapping.

That had been in Sunday's papers. Since then, the time she hadn't spent at board meetings she'd been on planes, commuting from New York to Boston and back. The wedding had been canceled quietly by her mother, who had called each of the invited guests. Claudia had given them the same reason that the PR spin machine at Sheridan Trust had given the press: "The bride and groom had second thoughts.'' So far the press hadn't gotten wind of the details behind Jack's arrest or the fact that he'd been passing himself off as Richard Lawrence for years. Hopefully, by the time they did, the canceled wedding would be old news.

Two good things had come out of Jack's charade. Once told about it, the board of directors at Sheridan Trust had started to respect her. Not that they'd been pleased with what she'd revealed, but they seemed willing to give her credit for discovering Jack's true identity before the wedding. And they'd been quite impressed when she'd been able to tell them that the deal with Bradshaw Enterprises was going forward. Hamilton had thought she'd shown ''intelligence and spunk'' in dealing with her conniving bridegroom.

After one of the meetings, a board member had come up to her and said, ''You remind me of your grandmother.''

Swiveling in her chair, Tyler glanced up at the portrait of Isabelle Sheridan that hung over the fireplace. All her life she'd dreamed of becoming just like the woman in the picture. But now she wanted much more than that.

She wanted Nick, and tomorrow morning he was going to board a plane for California and start a new life there. A life he'd dreamed of. In the past two days, she'd reminded herself of that several times.

Tyler glanced at her phone. He hadn't called her once since they'd left the precinct that night. And she hadn't been able to reach him. Once when she'd tried Sam's office, he'd just left. Then she'd missed him again at his mother's shop. How did one contact a man who was without a phone or a pager or e-mail?

The knock at her door made her jump, but she was

even more startled when her mother walked in. It was the first time she could remember Claudia ever doing that. Rising, Tyler walked around her desk. "Is something wrong?"

"No. I came because I wanted to thank you for believing that Howard had nothing to do with Richard's...I mean, Jack's plot."

Tyler did something then that she hadn't done since she was a child. Moving forward, she took her mother's hands in hers. "You love him a great deal, don't you."

Claudia nodded. "Not in the same way I loved your father, but I'm the kind of woman who needs someone in her life. I couldn't explain that to you when you were eleven."

"Mom, you don't have to—"

"No, I'd like to explain, or at least try to. I know that you couldn't forgive me for marrying again so soon after your father's death. But I'm not strong like you are. I never was. If I were, I would have insisted that you stay with me even though you were unhappy with me." Pausing, Claudia glanced up at the portrait of Isabelle Sheridan. "But then, you probably wouldn't be standing here today, running this company. And that's what you've always wanted."

"Yes," Tyler said, turning to look at her grandmother's portrait. "That's what I've always thought I wanted."

Claudia studied her for a moment. "And now you're not so sure?"

"It's not enough." Tyler turned back to her mother. "What you said was true. I never approved of the way you lived your life. It seemed to me that you were too dependent on a man for your happiness. I didn't want to be that way. I didn't ever want to love someone that much because I was afraid I might lose them."

"The way we both lost your father. And now you're afraid of losing that handsome PI, aren't you?"

When Tyler nodded, Claudia moved to a nearby cabinet and filled two crystal brandy glasses from a decanter. After handing one to Tyler, she said, "Sit, and tell me everything."

Tyler did, beginning with the moment she'd walked into Nick's office and had seen him lying on that couch. Claudia listened, laughing at times, frowning at others, saying nothing but a few, pithy swear words when Tyler described the scene in the alley outside the dance club.

When Tyler was finished, they both sat in absolute silence for a moment. Then Claudia said, "What are you going to do about it?"

"I don't know. It's because of Nick that I have my dream. The board is beginning to trust me in spite of the wedding fiasco."

"Or because of it."

"I don't want to stand in the way of Nick having his dream. He has to get out of Manhattan, make a clean break from his PI business, if he ever wants to practice law. He's waited almost as long as I have to reach his goal."

"Do you love him?" Claudia asked.

"Yes. Yes, I do."

"Have you told him that?"

Tyler shook her head, and Claudia rose, taking her hands and pulling her toward the door.

"Where are we going?' Tyler asked.

"I'm driving you to the airport so you can fly to Boston and tell him not to go."

"And how am I going to do that?"

"You're going to say, *I love you*," Claudia said as she urged Tyler into the elevator. "Those three little words work miracles."

Tyler wasn't so sure. "I'm supposed to just blurt it out?"

Claudia rolled her eyes. "You'll think of something. You have to have inherited *something* from me."

SHE HADN'T THOUGHT OF A THING. That was the one thing Tyler was sure of as she got out of the cab at Henry's Place and saw Lucy running down the steps. The young girl stopped short in surprise when she saw Tyler.

"You're here!"

"I came to find Nick. Do you know where he is?"

"Sure. He's on the roof. Everybody's there to say goodbye." She took Tyler's hands and drew her toward the doors, then said, "Wait, I almost forgot. I have to tell his airport taxi to wait."

Panic knotted in Tyler's stomach as she watched Lucy rush to the taxi and deliver her message. "He's going to the airport?" she asked.

Lucy nodded as she drew Tyler with her into the lobby. "He's going to be so surprised to see you!" In the elevator, she gave Tyler a quick hug. "I'm so glad you're here!" Tyler was still absorbing the sweetness of the gesture when she stepped onto the roof.

"Look who I found," Lucy announced.

Tyler found herself completely surrounded by Romanos, all talking at once.

"...What a wonderful surprise!"

"...We were just talking about you."

It was Gina who hugged her first. "How can I thank you for sending Hamilton Bradshaw to the shop?"

Drawing back, Tyler smiled. "He's going to invest in your expansion?"

Gina nodded. "You've made my dream come true."

"No, your designs have made your dream come true," Tyler said. After that, she felt as if she were running a gauntlet as she was passed first to Grace and then on to Sam, Tony and A.J. Finally, she found herself facing Nick, and he didn't say a thing. Of all the Romanos, he appeared to be the most surprised to see her. Afraid to read what was in his eyes, she glanced away and saw luggage sitting a few feet away.

"You weren't supposed to go to California until Wednesday."

"I changed my mind," Nick said.

"I'll say he did," Sam put in with a laugh.

"Big time," A.J. added.

"That's enough," Gina said. "Nick and Tyler need to talk."

"But I haven't offered Tyler any pizza yet," Tony said. "We can't be rude."

"Later," Gina said firmly.

As Gina herded the family off the roof, Nick still said nothing. For the first time in his life, words were failing him. It had been fifty-six hours since he'd seen her and he'd counted each one. When she'd first stepped out of the elevator, she'd looked exactly as she had that first morning when she'd walked into his office—cool, unapproachable. The pale blue suit was unwrinkled, her hair smoothed back from her face. A cold ball of fear had immediately settled in his stomach, freezing him. The woman he'd held in his arms only a few days ago had disappeared. She'd changed into...her grand-mother.

"You were going to leave without saying goodbye," Tyler said as she fisted her hands on her hips. "You were just going to fly off into the sunset, weren't you."

The sudden heat in her eyes and voice had the relief flooding through him. "Tyler, I—"

"No! Don't deny it. Lucy told me the taxi downstairs is waiting to take you to the airport." She pointed to the luggage. "And you're obviously all packed."

"I can explain—"

She raised one hand, palm out. "No. I know what a good liar you can be on the spur of the moment. Don't waste your breath." She moved a step closer. "Do you know what I came here to do? I came here to tell you *I love you.*" She clenched her hands. *"I love you!"*

He reached for her at the same instant that her fist came in low and made a bull's-eye connection to his bruised rib. He grunted as he stumbled backward. But he knew it was the joy singing through him and not the punch that had knocked the breath out of him. No woman had ever gotten under his guard before. And she stood there, fists clenched at her side, looking like some avenging goddess dropped down from Mount Olympus. "You really are a marvel!"

"I'm also your partner. At least I thought I was. I—"

Grabbing both her wrists, he jerked her close and covered her mouth with his. She struggled for only a moment before she wrapped her arms around him and held tight. He hadn't tasted her for days, years it seemed. But after a moment, he reluctantly drew back. "We have to talk."

She nodded.

"Just promise you won't punch me again."

"Depends on what you say."

"Before I explain about that—" he gestured toward his luggage "—I have a story to tell you. A love story about a Sheridan and a Romano. They met when she came to the city on business, and the instant they did, they fell in love. In a fairy tale, they would have lived happily ever after. But in real life, there were a lot of obstacles that came between them. First, they came from very different backgrounds. She'd been born to wealth, and he'd had to work for everything he had. Then there was the fact that they lived in different cities. Probably the most important thing that kept them apart was that they each had this dream about what they'd always wanted to do with their lives. She had a duty, an obligation, to run her family's business. And he had a dream, too, one he wasn't ready to give up. So they didn't get to live happily ever after in the traditional sense. But they did find a way to be together. They met on weekends when they could each get away from their families and their businesses. She would fly into town and stay with him. No one at her company ever found out. Even her family didn't know. But when they met, they created this special world where nothing else mattered."

Tyler clasped her hands tightly together. She felt cold. If she tried to talk, she was sure her teeth were going to chatter. The picture he painted was a logical solution to all of their problems. So why did she feel the same way she did when she was trapped in her nightmare? Why did she feel as if her heart was breaking? She had to find a way to tell him.

"That was the way your grandmother and my uncle Henry solved their problems."

Tyler blinked and stared at him. "My grandmother and your uncle Henry?"

"You wanted to know about the work I did for Belle Sheridan. Every time she came to New York, my job was to deliver her here to this hotel without anyone knowing about it. They lived this way for almost fifteen years."

Tyler tried to imagine what it must have been like— the secrecy, the stolen moments. Very romantic but...

"It's not my kind of solution," Nick said. "I could never be happy with a commuter relationship."

"You couldn't?"

"How about you?"

Tyler studied him then, trying to see in his eyes what he was thinking. But then, he'd told her already, hadn't he? He'd rather have no loaf at all than settle for only half. And now he was asking what she was willing to settle for. Throwing her arms around him, she said, "I don't want you to go." She felt his arms tighten around her until she could barely breathe. "But I'm not going to ask you to stay. It's not fair to you," she said. Feeling his hold on her slacken, she drew back so that she could see his face. "I thought we could work something out."

He looked at her closely. "You don't have a plan?"

She shook her head. "I can plan everything else. But this..." Pausing, she shook her head again as if to clear it. "I can't ask you to give up your dream. I promised myself that I wouldn't. How about if I do the commuting? I can use Sheridan Trust's private jet. People do have bicoastal relationships. And it certainly wouldn't be kept a secret."

"No. I promised myself that I would never repeat my uncle Henry's mistake of having a woman in his life only part time."

Tyler felt her heart contract.

"So *I* came up with a plan," Nick continued.

"You did?"

"I'm not moving to California. I'm moving to Boston, instead."

Tyler stared at him.

"You don't like it? I think it's perfect. I wanted to practice law in a place where I don't have a reputation as a PI, and Boston would fit the bill. My mother and my sisters are thrilled. Compared to L.A., Boston's practically in their backyard. They've already checked bus and plane schedules."

He looked pleased as punch. His eyes were filled with amusement. She narrowed hers. "As plans go, I think it's a little sketchy."

"Yeah, I figured you'd say that." He drew in a deep breath as his expression sobered. "But I'm planning on marrying a woman who *lives* to make plans. Did I forget to mention that?"

It wasn't laughter she saw in his eyes anymore. It was something that was the mirror image of what she was feeling. If her heart had contracted before, she could feel it expand now. "Yes," she managed.

"*Yes*, I forgot to mention it, or *yes*, you'll marry me?"

"Yes. Yes to both." Drawing him close, she held him as tightly as he'd held her a few moments before. "It's a beautiful plan."

He drew her away from him, but his hands still gripped her. "No. You were right the first time. It's a little sketchy. I'm counting on you to fill in the long-term details. Like where we're going to live—and how we're going to eat. We should probably hire a cook. And kids—how many to have and how soon."

Tyler swallowed hard. "Kids?"

"I want them," Nick said.

"Me, too." As she spoke the words, she discovered they were true. Her heart felt as if it were going to burst as she linked her arms around his neck. "And since I'm marrying a man who's very good at handling the here and now, why don't we get started?"

Nick's smile grew into laughter as he picked her up and spun her around and around. "I love a woman who has a plan." Then setting her down, he said, "I love you, Tyler Sheridan."

"I love you, too, Nick Romano," she said. Then drawing him close, she poured her love into the kiss.

* * *

*If you liked this PERSONAL TOUCH
book then you'll love
MS TAKEN
by Jo Leigh—on the shelves next month.*

Modern Romance™
...seduction and
passion guaranteed

Tender Romance™
...love affairs that
last a lifetime

Sensual Romance™
...sassy, sexy and
seductive

Blaze
...sultry days and
steamy nights

Medical Romance™
...medical drama on
the pulse

Historical Romance™
...rich, vivid and
passionate

29 new titles every month.

*With all kinds of Romance for
every kind of mood...*

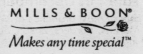

MILLS & BOON®

Makes any time special™

MAT4

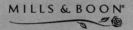

Sensual Romance™

MS TAKEN by Jo Leigh

The Personal Touch

Secretly in love with her boss, Jane Dobson isn't expecting to grab his attention by getting hit on the head! But now Jane thinks he's her fiancé and Charles can't think of *any* reason why he should try and change her mind...especially when she wants to start the honeymoon early!

CHANCE ENCOUNTER by Jill Shavis

Men of Chance

The last thing TJ Chance needs is to be responsible for Ally Wheeler—a timid city girl who thinks he is the ticket to a brand-new life. Of course, if she's looking for a wild time, he can certainly deliver...*in more ways than one.*

ONE EAGER BRIDE TO GO by Pamela Burford

The Wedding Ring

Sunny is dubious when her friends set her up with an old flame, but her doubts soon disappear. Except Kirk has news that Sunny doesn't want to hear—he's not really looking for romance...but he just can't seem to keep Sunny *out of his bed!*

SEDUCED by Janelle Denison

Stealing

Ryan Matthews wants sexy Jessica Newman, but there's something holding her back. So now Ryan has decided that it's time to launch a sensual assault and he isn't above tempting her with her own forbidden fantasies to do it...

On sale 7th December 2001

Available at most branches of WH Smith, Tesco, Martins, Borders, Eason, Sainsbury's, and most good paperback bookshops.

0801/123/MB19

OTHER NOVELS BY

PENNY JORDAN

POWER GAMES

POWER PLAY

CRUEL LEGACY

TO LOVE, HONOUR & BETRAY

THE HIDDEN YEARS

THE PERFECT SINNER

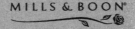

MILLS & BOON®

FREE!

2 Books
and a surprise gift!

We would like to take this opportunity to thank you for reading this Mills & Boon® book by offering you the chance to take TWO more specially selected titles from the Sensual Romance™ series absolutely FREE! We're also making this offer to introduce you to the benefits of the Reader Service™—

- ★ FREE home delivery
- ★ FREE gifts and competitions
- ★ FREE monthly Newsletter
- ★ Books available before they're in the shops
- ★ Exclusive Reader Service discounts

Accepting these FREE books and gift places you under no obligation to buy; you may cancel at any time, even after receiving your free shipment. Simply complete your details below and return the entire page to the address below. **You don't even need a stamp!**

YES! Please send me 2 free Sensual Romance books and a surprise gift. I understand that unless you hear from me, I will receive 4 superb new titles every month for just £2.49 each, postage and packing free. I am under no obligation to purchase any books and may cancel my subscription at any time. The free books and gift will be mine to keep in any case.

TIZEB

Ms/Mrs/Miss/Mr ....Initials ....
BLOCK CAPITALS PLEASE

Surname ....

Address ....

....

....Postcode ....

Send this whole page to:
UK: The Reader Service, FREEPOST CN81, Croydon, CR9 3WZ
EIRE: The Reader Service, PO Box 4546, Kilcock, County Kildare (stamp required)

Offer not valid to current Reader Service subscribers to this series. We reserve the right to refuse an application and applicants must be aged 18 years or over. Only one application per household. Terms and prices subject to change without notice. Offer expires 31st May 2002. As a result of this application, you may receive offers from other carefully selected companies. If you would prefer not to share in this opportunity please write to The Data Manager at the address above.

Mills & Boon® is a registered trademark owned by Harlequin Mills & Boon Limited.
Sensual Romance™ is being used as a trademark.